TREASURE ISLAND

Retold by Lila K. Huron-Albinger

CONTENTS

CHAPTER   PAGE

1   The Captain   2

2   Black Dog and Black Spots   16

3   Billy Bones's Secret   34

4   The Launch of the Adventure   56

5   The Launch of the Hispaniola   80

6   The Secret Plot for Treasure Island   94

7   Unexpected Company   110

8   The Doctor's Tale   120

9   Jim Returns   136

10   The Start of My Sea Adventure   156

11   Captain Hawkins   172

12   Nightmare in Real Life   190

13   Another Black Spot   202

14   The Search for Flint's Fist   214

15   The End of the Adventure   230

CHAPTER 1

The Captain

I was asked by Dr. Livesey, Squire Trelawney, and the rest of the survivors to record the story of Treasure Island. They wanted me to tell the whole tale from start to finish, leaving out only the exact location of the island, for there is buried treasure still there. The tale starts in the year 17—, when my parents owned the Admiral Benbow Inn, and the old sailor with the scarred cheek arrived to stay with us.

The memory of his arrival is still vivid and I can see him trudging steadily toward our door. His only belongings were in an old sailor's chest brought by a man with a wheelbarrow. The seaman was tall and large, sun-burned from his voyages, and appeared strong despite his advancing years. A long, ratty pig-tail hung down his back. As he got closer, I could see his hands bore the marks of many battles, and he had a stark white scar running across one cheek. He looked around as he plodded along, sometimes whistling and some-times singing. He often sang that old sailors' song about "Yo-ho-hum, and a bottle of rum!" in a voice that had seen too much drink and too many bars.

When he reached our door, he knocked with the handspike that sailors carry, a wooden stick covered with iron. My father answered his call and the old man asked for a glass of rum. He savored it slowly, all the time looking around at the bay and the surrounding cliffs. He glanced at our sign hanging above him, and finally asked if we had many visitors.

"I wish we did," replied my father. "It gets lonely up here."

"That suits me fine," said the old sailor. "You there!" he said to the delivery man. "Help me carry that chest upstairs!" He turned back to my father. "I'm a simple man with plain tastes. I want to be left alone, and I want to watch the sea. You can call me Captain."

He threw down a few gold coins for payment, telling my father to ask him for more when those had been used up. The expression on his face was so forbidding we dared not argue. Although dressed in rags, he still had the commanding manner of a captain or skipper, not that of a simple deckhand.

After carrying the chest to the man's room, the delivery man recounted how the old sailor had come on the mail coach, asking about the availability of lodging along the coast.

"Your inn attracted his attention," he said. "It seems isolated, clean, and well run." He could tell us nothing more about our visitor.

In the following days we found the captain to be very quiet, staying at the shore or on the

cliffs, watching the sea with his telescope. In the evenings he sat by the fire drinking rum and water, mixed very strong. Even when spoken to he would usually stay silent, glowering at the person interrupting his thoughts. He had an annoying habit of blowing through his nose and it sounded like a foghorn. So most of us learned to avoid him.

He would return each day and ask if any sailing men had passed through. We thought at first he was lonely, but then we began to realize that he didn't want to meet anyone. Sometimes men would stop on their way to the Bristol coast. The captain would peek at them from the glass in the parlor door before entering the room. If he did enter, he would remain utterly silent.

I was the only one who knew his secret. One day he took me aside and promised me a silver fourpenny piece each month if I kept a lookout for a sailor with one leg. I was to notify him at once if such a person appeared.

Sometimes he was reluctant to pay me my wage and would stare at me and blow his nose. Two or three days later, he would reconsider and again ask me to do the job and give me my coin.

I don't know which of us feared this one-legged man more, for I began to see him in my dreams. Sometimes, the leg was cut off at the knee, sometimes at the hip. Occasionally I dreamed of a horrible creature who only had one leg growing out of the center of his body. This monster was never hindered by his lack of two legs, but was able to chase me over ditches and hedges with ease. Even though I never had to warn the captain of such a visitor, I felt I earned my pay with my nightmares.

Even haunted by the dreams, I came to fear the captain less than anyone else who knew him. Sometimes when he drank too much, he would sing the old wild sea songs, unaware of the reactions of those around him. Other times, he would order a glass of ale for everyone. Then all our guests would have to sit and listen to his tales and songs, joining in on the choruses. The neighbors were terrified, fearing they would come to some harm. They would try to outdo each other in their singing, lest he take offense at the level of their participation. If he was not satisfied, his hand would strike the table with great force, and he would roar for silence. He would not allow our guests to leave until he had fallen asleep or gone to bed.

His stories were horrible and frightened all the neighbors. He talked about hangings and men walking the plank. He told tales of pirates on the Spanish Main and the Dry Tortugas. All were sure he had been with some of the worst and cruel men cruising on the seas, and his language was so crude the neighbors were shocked. My father feared the reputation of our establishment would be destroyed. I, however, believed that the people who came to listen to the captain's tales took a perverse pleasure in them, for these stories provided some

excitement to their simple lives. Some of the younger men even seemed to admire him, feeling he was the type of sailor who upheld England's reputation as the most feared nation on the high seas.

In only one way did he really harm us. He continued to live at the inn long after his rent money was used up. Whenever my father tried to ask for more, he would receive one of those fierce stares. My father, whose health was not good, would leave the room quite upset, his courage gone.

While living with us, the captain never changed his clothing except to buy some stockings from a vendor. His hat was in such bad shape that the brim hung down in his face, but he did nothing to fix it. His coat was full of patches he had sewn himself. He received no letters and sent none himself and never spoke to any of our neighbors unless he was drunk. No one had ever seen his big sea chest opened.

The only time someone actually defied him was toward the end of his life and that of my father's. Dr. Livesey had come to see my father and stayed to eat dinner with us. While waiting for his horse to be brought around, the doctor went into the parlor to smoke his pipe. He and the captain made quite a contrast. The doctor was nicely dressed and the captain looked very much the pirate, sitting drunk at the table singing his favorite song:

Fifteen men on the dead
mate's trunk—
Yo-ho-hum, and a bottle full of rum!
Booze and the devil finished
every last one—
Yo-ho-hum, and a bottle of rum!

I no longer feared the captain's songs as I once did, so this was new only to the doctor, and I could see he was not impressed.

Our gardener was in the room, and the doctor talked with the man about his health.

He did so until the captain slapped his hand
on the table for silence. Since Dr. Livesey had
not seen this performance before he kept on
talking. This caused the captain to glare at the
doctor and he hit the table harder and harder.

"Stifle it!" he roared. "Be still!"

"Sir, were you talking to me?" asked the
doctor in a deadpan voice. When the captain
swore at him and told him yes, the doctor continued. "I will tell you one thing! The world
will soon be rid of a nasty villain if you continue to drink like that!"

The captain was furious and jumped up,
pulling open his knife and promising to hang
the doctor on the wall.

Dr. Livesey was unmoved and addressed
him as before, over his shoulder and not changing the tone of his voice. His words carried
throughout the room so that all could hear.

"I recommend you put that knife away at
this instant, for I vow that you will hang at the
next court session."

The two of them stared at each other, neither of them moving a muscle. The captain finally gave in and put the knife away and sat down again in his seat.

The doctor continued. "Now that I know what kind of character you are, I will have to keep an eye on you at all times, for I am also a magistrate. If I hear of any complaints against you, I will use my authority to find you and remove you from this area. Take heed to my warning!"

Dr. Livesey left not long after, and the captain gave us no further trouble for many days.

CHAPTER 2

Black Dog and
Black Spots

A few days later the story began to get really interesting. Winter was on us; long, very cold days and many storms. We did not have much hope for my father. His health was rapidly getting worse. It was left to my mother and me to do all of the work around the inn and to nurse my father as well. As a result, we did not have much time to worry about the captain.

Early on a very cold January morning, the captain got up earlier than normal and, as usual, went out to the shore with his telescope.

My mother was still upstairs with my father and I was setting the table for the captain's breakfast. When the parlor door opened I saw a pale, thin man step in. He was missing two fingers on his left hand and carried a knife used by sailors called a cutlass. Its curved blade looked out of place by his side for he did not appear to have the courage of a fighter. Since I had been expecting a seaman with one leg, this man took me by surprise. Though he did not look like a sailor, he still seemed to carry the air of the sea with him.

When I asked if he wanted something to drink, he requested some rum. As I went to fetch it, he stopped me and asked me to come near.

"Is this where my shipmate Bill sits?" he asked with a sneer on his face.

"There is no one here by that name, sir," I replied. "Our only guest is a man we call the captain."

"Hmm, that sounds about right," he replied. "His cheek has a long scar on it, and he tends to be loud when he gets drunk. Let's see, the scar is on the right cheek. Now boy, where is he?"

I told him the captain was out on his daily walk and showed him the way. He asked a few more questions and wanted to know when the captain would return. He said his presence would be like a shot of rum to the captain, but I was not so sure. He continued to leer at me. I was sure he was up to no good, but it was not really my concern for the captain had not warned me about this man at all. I was still looking for the one-legged man.

I wondered whether I should try to warn the captain, but the man waited just inside our door, taking a quick peek around the edge every now and again. When I tried to leave the building, he called me back, swearing at me one minute and then sweetly calling me a good lad. He told me I reminded him of his own son. He was thoroughly unpleasant.

Soon we could see the captain coming up the road. "Quick, mate!" he said. "I want to surprise him. You're coming with me. We'll hide here behind this door."

With his hand on my shoulder I did not have much choice. I soon found myself stuck in the corner behind the door right beside the stranger. I was becoming quite frightened, especially since I could see the stranger was scared himself. He had his hand on his cutlass, ready to draw.

The captain walked in, closed the door behind him with a slam, and sat down to his breakfast.

"Bill," said our new visitor in a voice that was supposed to be booming

The captain turned around and the color drained out of his face. I felt a moment's pity, for I saw in front of me an elderly, ill man.

"Black Dog!" he cried.

"That's right," Black Dog replied. "I came back to see you, my mate. We've certainly been through a lot together, haven't we, since I lost these two!" And he held up his mangled hand.

"What do you want, Black Dog?" asked the captain. "Hurry up, be quick!"

Black Dog asked me for some rum and sat down across from the captain, sitting sideways to keep one eye on his mate and one on the door. He told me to leave, but to keep the door wide open and warned me not to listen at the keyhole.

I left for the dining room, but I must admit I tried to listen as best I could. After a while, their voices grew louder and I could hear the captain swearing.

"Enough, enough!" cried the captain suddenly. "If it's to be a hanging, we all hang, I say!"

At once, I heard a loud noise as the table and chair crashed over. The captain was shouting. I heard the sound of steel on steel, followed by a cry of pain, and suddenly Black Dog came streaking by me out the door. The captain was hot on his heels, and both had their knives drawn. Black Dog had a cut on his shoulder and blood was pouring out. When they reached the door, the captain threw his cutlass, which could have surely killed Black Dog, but it hit the sign above the entrance.

That finished the fight. Black Dog took to his heels down the road while the captain had only the strength to look at our sign in confusion. Finally he turned and came inside and unsteadily caught himself from falling against the doorframe. "Get me a drink, Jim!" he cried unsteadily. "I've got to leave now! My drink!"

My nerves were not steady but after a few tries, I managed to pour a glass. Suddenly, I heard something fall and ran in to find the captain lying on the floor. My mother came running down the stairs, and we were able to raise his head and see that he was still breathing.

"Oh, what are we going to do?" she moaned. "We are ruined for sure! It's too much with your father sick!"

We had no idea what to do. The captain looked terrible and sounded worse. When we tried to force some of the drink into him, his teeth would not open. We were profoundly relieved to see Dr. Livesey enter to visit my father.

He examined the captain and told us he had suffered a stroke. "Mrs. Hawkins, you go on up to your husband. Try not to let him know what has happened. I'll be up as soon as possible to see him. Jim can help me here. This fellow's hardly worth it, but I must try to save his life. Jim, I need a bowl."

I brought the bowl as requested and the doctor tore the captain's shirt sleeve, exposing the large inside vein. We could see several tattoos, including one with a gallows and man hanging from it. "Appropriate, I should think," he said touching the tattoo. "Now, Jim, are you bothered by the sight of blood? No? Good then. I will tell you what I want you to do."

He instructed me on how he wanted me to help him and opened the vein. He took a great deal of blood before the captain recovered consciousness. The old man recognized the doctor with a scowl, but looked glad to see me. He tried to sit up and asked where Black Dog had gone.

The doctor told him the villain had gone. He admonished the captain that he would have to stop his drinking or the next stroke would be fatal. The doctor and I managed to get him to his bed. Dr. Livesey took me aside and told me to keep an eye on him; he would probably be in bed for about a week. Another stroke would finish him off.

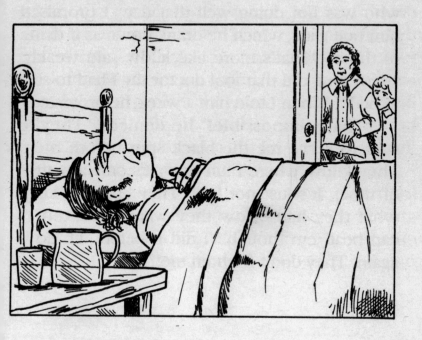

At lunchtime I took up his meal and some medicine ordered by the doctor. The captain was still in bed, but very anxious to see me and desperate for a drink. "You've got to bring me something, Jim! No, don't tell me what the doctor said! What does he know? Nobody cares about me! You're the best one here. I know you'll help me, right, Jim? I'm sure I'll die without a glass of rum!" He went on and on, and I was concerned for both him and my father, who was not doing well that day. I promised him one glass, which he drank down as if dying of thirst. "That's more like it," he said weakly. "How long did that fool doctor say I had to stay in bed?" When I told him a week, he protested.

"That's impossible!" he denied. "They're sure to serve me the black spot before then. They know where I am now; it's only a matter of time. It's just not fair! They couldn't keep what they had. Now they want mine, too. I can beat 'em though. I did it before, I'll do it again. They don't frighten me!"

I had no idea what he was talking about. During this tirade, he tried to sit up and get to his feet, using my shoulder as his crutch. He gripped it so hard I was sure he would break it. I knew if I moved he would fall again and then we would have to get him back in bed. The tone of his voice showed how weak he was, for all his fighting words had no strength to back them up.

Sitting only made him dizzy and he lay back down, exhausted. After a few moments he started to talk again. "Did you see that man?" he asked feebly.

"Do you mean Black Dog?" I questioned.

"That's him," he agreed. "He may be a scoundrel, but the rest are worse. I need to tell you. They'll probably give me the black spot seeing how I can't escape this place. If they come, I want you to ride to the doctor's and fetch him. They'll be after that sea trunk in the corner. Tell the doctor to bring the authorities, 'cus old Flint's crew will be here

27

for me. Flint was our captain. I was first mate, but I'm the only one who knows the exact location. When he was dying he gave it to me, just like I am now. But don't you do anything unless they give me the black spot, or Black Dog appears, or the man with one leg comes. Him 'specially, Jim! Understand?"

I did not. I asked him what the black spot was, and he told me it was a summons. He

promised to tell me if he got it, and I was to keep my eyes open for him. None the wiser, I watched and listened for a little while, until he finally fell asleep.

I was unsure what to do and whether to tell Dr. Livesey the whole disjointed story. My biggest fear was that the captain would wake up and be furious that I had told anyone. Events took their own course, however, for my father died that evening, and I had no chance to think about the captain.

The next morning, the captain was able to come down for his meals, but his appetite was not large. In the confusing state of affairs, I confess he simply helped himself to as much rum as he wanted for we were busy dealing with my father's death and funeral. The night before the funeral, the captain was sitting downstairs drunk, singing at the top of his lungs, showing total disrespect for my mother.

We could do nothing, since we were still afraid of him even though he was very weak.

There was no one to help us and Dr. Livesey was away on another case.

The captain no longer had the strength to go out, but would take his meals and step outside for a moment to smell the air. He was in more of a foul mood than ever, and usually had his cutlass sitting on the table before him. Even so, he seemed to withdraw more and more into himself and took no notice of others around him.

The day after my father's funeral I was standing outside for a moment in bitterly cold air, mourning my loss. Presently I saw somebody coming toward us down the road. He was blind, tapping a stick in front of him and wore an enormous hood over his head and eyes. On his back was a decrepit old sea-cloak and he looked like a beggar. When he drew near, he asked in a high faltering voice for someone to tell him where he was. When I told him he was at the Admiral Benbow Inn, he asked me to take his arm and help him in. He took my arm and held it with a vise-like grip. Even though I recoiled, he held it firmly, leaving me with no choice but to help him. He pulled me closer and demanded I take him to the captain. When I refused, he threatened to break my arm and twisted it so hard I cried out.

"But, sir!" I cried. "The captain is not of sound mind anymore. I am afraid for you, for he now carries his cutlass drawn at all times. Someone else..."

The blind man interrupted and demanded to be taken anyway. His voice sounded so inhuman I was more afraid of his words than his grip.

"Take me to him," he demanded. "When he comes in, tell him he has an old friend to see him."

He gave my arm another horrible wrench and threatened again to break it completely. I knew I had more to fear from this man than the captain. I opened the door to the parlor and repeated the words in a quavering voice.

The captain looked around and was instantly sober. He did not look frightened but very sick. He tried to stand up but did not have the strength.

The blind man told him to stay put, and instructed him to hold out his right hand, palm up. I saw the blind man put something into the captain's hand, and the captain closed his hand around it.

The next instant, the blind man turned and left, making his way to the door as if he had sight. When we got up to look, he was already off in the distance, making his way down the road, tapping with his stick.

The captain took a moment to look at the palm of his hand, turning over the black spot of paper resting there. He stood up as if to flee, crying something about ten o'clock and having six more hours. But he fell at once onto the floor, clutching his throat.

Calling for my mother, I ran to him but it was too late. The captain was dead. I reacted by starting to cry, for even though I had not liked him, his death came close on the heels of my father's and I was still in shock.

CHAPTER 3

Billy Bones's Secret

I told my mother everything that had happened and what the captain had told me.
We knew we had a problem. The captain
had not paid us for some time, so we had a
rightful claim to some of his money. I knew
we would see none of it if we did not retrieve
it before the captain's "friends" returned. If I
obeyed the seaman's wishes and went to find
Dr. Livesey, my mother would be left alone.
Neither of us thought it was wise to let her
face those men on her own.

The house was full of sounds: clocks tick-
ing, the coal in the fire grate dropping; and we
were sure we could hear footsteps all the

time. We had a dead man at our feet and we knew the blind man could not be far away. We finally decided to try to ask for help from our neighbors. We left at once without even putting on our coats to protect us from the weather.

The village lay a small distance from us in the opposite direction from where the blind man had gone, a fact that reassured me. As we ran, we were glad to hear no unusual sounds behind us or find any surprises waiting up ahead.

As it was twilight, we were relieved to see lighted windows, but each house greeted us the same. No one would come to our aid, and all seemed reluctant to even have anything to do with us. Several had seen unsavory characters on the road the last couple of days. We heard reports of one small ship, or lugger, which was similar to a pirate ship, that had been seen at an isolated cove called Kitt's Hole. This was enough to scare any of the neighbors, although several volunteered to go to fetch the doctor on our behalf. We could not wait, and as incredible as it must have seemed, my mother was adamant to return to get our portion of the money.

All the villagers thought we were out of our heads, but we went back. They gave us each a loaded gun and told us they would have some horses saddled in case we needed to flee. One boy was sent to find the doctor.

The trip back to the inn was worse than the trip to the village. We knew that at least we were going home to a dead man, but we had no way of knowing whether the others had gotten there first. The moon was full and offered us no protection from being seen, but we did our best to slip beside what buildings and hedges we could find.

We entered and I locked the door. Lighting a candle, we went into the parlor. The captain was lying where we had left him, his eyes still open and one arm stretched out to the side.

"Quick, Jim," my mother said, "close the blinds. We don't need any spying eyes. Good, now come help me. I sure hate to touch him!" We knelt beside him, for we had to find the key to his sea chest. Beside his hand was the small piece of paper, black on one side. I knew this was the dreaded "black spot." On the reverse were the words telling him he had until ten o'clock this evening.

This was reassuring to my mother when I told her, for it was only six o'clock now. I searched his pockets but found only his small knife, a little tobacco, and his compass. This was no help to us at all, and my mother suggested we see if the key was around his neck.

With a great deal of loathing, I opened his shirt and found the key there on an old string. I had to use his own knife to cut the string, but we soon had the key and left him where he lay and went upstairs.

The chest, which was very plain except for a "B" branded on the top, showed wear from many years of use. My mother took the key and we lifted the lid and looked inside. The inside smelled strongly of tobacco, and we found a new suit of clothes lying on top in beautiful shape, neatly folded. Beneath was an assortment of odds and ends, nothing special, and we moved these out of our way. After another old cloak, we found a package covered in oilcloth and a cloth bag that jingled with gold when we picked it up.

My mother opened the bag and began to search for the right coins, for there were coins from many different countries.

"I'll not take more than I'm owed," she said, so we spent several precious minutes sorting the coins.

Suddenly I could hear in the winter quiet the blind man's stick. He knocked on the door and tried to open it. I was very glad I had thought to lock it. Silence. Then we heard the tapping recede, until he finally disappeared, much to our great relief.

"Please, mother, take the whole thing! We've got to get out of here!"

She would not listen. I was afraid the blind man would be skeptical of the locked door and would return before ten o'clock. She was still at her counting, when a few minutes later we heard a quiet whistle down the hill. Now we knew we had no time to lose.

"I think I have enough," she said.

She took the coins she had counted and put them in her pocket. I grabbed the oilskin bundle, which we hadn't opened yet. Leaving the candle upstairs, we silently felt our way down the steps and left the inn. As the fog slowly lifted around us, we made our way as fast as we could. Concealed by the last stray wisps, we could hear the sound of many footsteps running toward the inn. Someone carried a light.

"Run, Jim! Run! Take these coins and go! I think I'm going to faint!"

I was sure this would mean our death, and I swore at the villagers for being such cowards.

41

My mother had not helped by insisting she get only her share. I wished again she had just taken the whole packet; then we would have had time to escape. Not too gently, I managed to get her to the side of the road, where I laid her down in the ditch. I hid under the arch of the bridge—it was the best I could do—and hoped and prayed we would not be discovered.

Even though I was thoroughly frightened, I placed myself in a good spot behind some bushes to watch what was happening at our home. Soon eight men arrived, led by the man with the lantern. In the middle I could see the blind man giving instructions to the rest to take down the door by force.

Great was their surprise to find the door unlocked when they crashed inside. The blind man urged them on, his voice becoming more excited and enraged, swearing at them for going too slow.

Five went in, while two stayed outside with the blind man.

"He's dead!" they cried.

"Then someone go through his pockets! The rest of you go get the chest!"

A few moments later the upstairs window broke and one of them stuck his head out.

"Someone got here first, Pew!" he yelled. "Everything's been searched and thrown out!"

"I want to know if it's there!" shrieked Pew, the blind man.

Pew was furious when he found out only the money was left behind. "I want to know if Flint's parcel is there!" he screamed.

"I can't see Flint's fist anywhere!" was the reply.

The man downstairs told Pew the same news, that Bill had already had his pockets turned out.

"It must be the people who lived here, that boy and his mother! I should have hurt him when I had the chance. The door was locked a few minutes ago. Spread out! Look for them! They can't be far!" Pew was greatly excited.

The men trashed our home searching for us until they were satisfied we were not inside. When they emerged to look outside we all heard the long whistle I had heard before. It seemed to be a signal that danger was coming, and they all wanted to run for their lives.

"Keep going you fools!" he roared. "Find those people! I'd give anything to have working eyes again!" A few made a show of looking, but they were not interested in sticking around for much longer.

In a ferocious rage, Pew started to hit them with his stick, and they swore at him and tried to stop him. While they were fighting among themselves, the villagers finally came to our rescue on horses. When the pirates saw what was happening, they turned and fled. Pew was left standing there on his own in the middle of the road swearing after them.

"Black Dog, Johnny, Dirk! Don't you dare leave me, you fools! Come back!" he cried.

He had no chance. The horses bore down on him in the dark and he was trampled to death in the road. I jumped up from my hiding spot and ran to call to the drivers. They stopped, realizing they had hit something.

The riders were revenue officers brought by the boy who was sent to fetch Dr. Livesey. He had returned as soon as he could. My mother and I owed our lives to him, for surely the pirates would have found us in short order.

The blind man was pronounced dead. After the men had carried my mother to the village, she was revived with no harm done, although she regretted she still had not collected her fair share of the captain's money.

The supervisor sent a couple of his men off to Kitt's Hole when they told him the news. Unfortunately they found the little ship already under sail, so none of the villains were captured. Another man was sent to warn the

King's ship down the coast to prevent any mischief from coming to it.

When I went back to our little inn, I was appalled at the havoc the men had wrought. They had made quite a mess, but the only things taken were the captain's money and the coins we had in our till. I knew we could not continue staying at the inn. The supervisor, Mr. Dance, could not understand what they had been looking for.

"I think they were looking for this," I replied, showing him the bundle hidden in my jacket pocket. "I think it needs to be put somewhere very safe."

We decided I would hold on to it, and all of us would go back to Dr. Livesey's house. We set forth at once.

We found the doctor at the squire's Hall. Mr. Dance and I were taken to the library where we found Squire Trelawney and the doctor. It was the first time I had seen the squire up close, and I was surprised at how tall he was. He was a well-travelled man and his face was full of life and wit. "Hello there, Mr. Dance," said the squire. "What brings you and the boy here tonight?"

The supervisor told them our story and the two men listened with great amazement. When it was all told, the squire congratulated Mr. Dance on a job well done, informing him that he had nothing to worry about in the trampling death of the blind beggar Pew. He sent for some ale to quench our thirst and then Mr. Dance was allowed to go home.

"Jim, do you still have the bundle after all?" asked the doctor. I gave it to him. He looked at it for some time without opening it, turning it over and over in his hands. Then he put it in his pocket.

While I was eating some supper they began to talk of Flint. "I've heard of him," said the squire. "He is said to be the most blood-thirsty pirate that sailed the high seas. He is worse than Blackbeard. Even the Spanish are afraid of him. The only good thing about him is he is an Englishman. I saw his ship once off of Trinidad. The captain of my boat was so afraid he turned around and put back into harbor."

The doctor had heard of this villain too. He wondered if the parcel I had taken might have some clue as to the location of Flint's hoard. No one knew what size the treasure would be.

"Let's open it and see," exclaimed the squire. If it tells us the location of the treasure, I will find a ship and outfit it at my expense. You and I, and young Jim Hawkins, here, will sail off to find the treasure, no matter how long it takes." With my permission, the doctor began to open the bundle.

Inside were a small book and a paper sealed with wax. Together we looked at the book first. The first page held only idle doodles on it, with phrases such as I had seen on the captain's tattoos. The next bunch of pages held what looked at first glance, like a ledger.

50

Where the descriptions would have been written were a series of small crosses between the numbers. On several lines were the names of places, or latitude and longitude markers.

These entries spanned more than twenty years and showed how the dead man's balance had grown larger and larger. At the end was the notation, "B. Bones, his share."

Dr. Livesey was confused. The squire reasoned that the entries showed the names of ships and places the pirate had sunk or ransacked, and the recording of his share of the booty. They could see that as his wealth had increased, so had the captain's rank on ship. There was little else in the book of importance, except a table at the end listing common equivalences of French, Spanish, and English money. The captain had been correct. He was a frugal man who would not allow himself to be cheated.

The doctor now turned to the sealed paper and broke the wax carefully. It was a detailed map complete with longitude and latitude. The geography of this island was clearly marked. It also listed instructions on how to sail to the island and safely dock a ship. Not a large island, about five miles wide and nine miles long, it looked a little like a dragon sitting on its heels. The hill in the center was named Spy-glass and several notes had been added later. What stood out for us were the two red crosses on the north end of the island, and the single one on the southwest portion. To the side of this was the writing, "Here is most of treasure."

On the back was more writing:

Find giant tree at base of Spy-glass at N. of N. N. E. Look toward Skeleton Island E. S. E. and by E. Walk ten feet. Silver bar is in north spot, look to the lie of east knoll, 60 feet S. of dark cliff with face. Arms easy to find. Go to hill of sand N.

*point of cape on north cove, E. and
a quarter N.*

J. F.

That was it. Although I did not understand
a word, the two men were very excited.

Squire Trelawney wanted to start at once
and asked the doctor to wind up his affairs as
soon as he could. He would go to Bristol and
outfit a ship with everything we would need

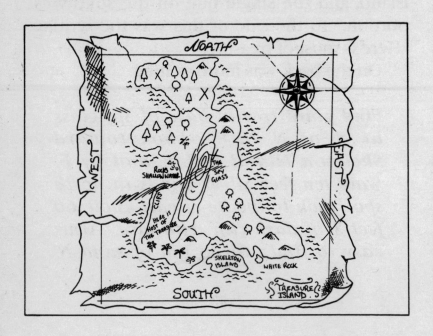

for the voyage. I, Jim Hawkins, would be the cabin boy, and Dr. Livesey would be the ship's doctor. The squire would take along his men Redruth, Joyce, and Hunter. He was positive we would all return wealthy for the rest of our days.

The doctor was all for the plan, except for one thing. He was afraid that the squire would not be able to keep our purpose a secret. If the rest of the pirates were to hear of our plan, they would be sure to make every effort to stop us and try to capture the map. We were to take every precaution, and I was to stay with the doctor all the time. Joyce and Hunter were to be the squire's bodyguards. All of us had to keep quiet.

"Dr. Livesey, you are right as usual," replied the squire. "I promise to tell no one!"

CHAPTER 4

The Launch of the Adventure

Things did not work out the way we had planned. Preparations for sailing took longer than expected. The doctor was not able to keep me with him, for he had to go to London to find someone to replace him. I moved into the squire's Hall under the watchful eye of Redruth, the gamekeeper. All of my movements were carefully monitored.

My dreams were full of sailing ships and deserted islands and wonderful adventures. I had the map with me and soon had every feature memorized. In my mind's eye, I explored every inch; in my daydreams I fought wild natives and fierce animals. All my imaginings did not prepare me for what really happened.

Finally, a letter arrived for Dr. Livesey that had a further instruction to be opened by me, Jim Hawkins, in the doctor's absence. Since he was away, Redruth and I opened it. It contained the following information:

Old Anchor Inn, Bristol
March 1, 17—

Greetings Livesey,

I am sending this to both London and the Hall, not knowing where you are. Our sailing ship is ready and waiting to sail. She is a sweet thing and will be easy to sail. Her weight is two hundred tons; her name, Hispaniola.

My old friend Blandly has been a great help and through him I purchased the ship. I have had lots of help from many others, especially when

*they heard the purpose of our trip—
treasure, I mean.*

I paused in my reading. I knew Dr. Livesey
would not be pleased when he read that, and
commented about it to Redruth. He was
under the impression that it was the squire's
right to talk freely. After that comment, I held
my peace, and finished the letter.

*Blandly got a very good price for the
ship. There seems to be a bunch of
men who dislike him intensely, thinking he would do anything for money.
The rumor is that the boat belonged to
him in the first place and he sold it to
me for more than it is worth, but I am
not about to believe these disgruntled
fellows. They all agree on one thing:
the absolute merits of the ship.*

*The pace of the refitting has gone very
slow, but I am satisfied everything is*

ready. The only problem I have found is with the crew.

I was hoping for a crew of twenty, in case we encounter unfriendly natives, pirates, or those horrible French. But I had a hard time finding even six. Finally I got a lucky break.

Standing on the dock, I started talking to another man passing the time. He told me he was a former sailor, but now kept an inn in Bristol. Now that his health was not as good on land, he was looking for a job as a cook on a ship. He knew many other sailing men in town and could help me to find able men for our voyage. He had hobbled down that morning to smell again the sea.

I was moved a great deal to hear his story, and I hired him on the spot to be our cook. His name is Long John Silver, and he has one leg, the other lost in the service of the famous Hawke. I felt this to be such a recommendation of his bravery, I was compelled to help him if I could. He is one of those poor souls with no pension—I can't imagine what this world is coming to, Livesey!

With his help, we found the rest of the crew. They are true sea-salts with lots of experience between them. They look like sailors, rough and tough, but with great courage if we need it.

Long John fired two of the men I had hired, believing them to be too soft for the job, saying we needed the value of experience for such a trip.

I am doing fine. I seem to have enormous energy and am eating like an elephant, and sleeping like a baby. Oh how I am looking forward to sailing! Off to sea we go! I can hardly wait!

Hurry, Livesey! Allow Hawkins to visit with his mother, taking Redruth as his bodyguard, then both of them come at once to Bristol!

John Trelawney

P. S. By the way—I have instructed Blandly to send another ship to search for us if we have not returned by the end of August.

Our captain is a fine man, although not very friendly. Long John found a man to be first mate by the name of Arrow. Out boatswain plays the pipes, so we will have a fine tune as we set sail.

I forgot to mention that I found that Silver has a very healthy bank account,

*and has never been overdrawn. His
wife will manage the inn, and having
seen her, you and I would probably
guess that she is one reason he is so
willing to go back to sea!*

J.T.

*P.P.S. Allow Hawkins to stay overnight
with his mother.*

J.T.

This letter was just what I wanted to hear.
Redruth did his best to take away my excitement, always complaining and whining.

We left the next morning for my old home
and found my mother doing very well, especially since the captain was no longer there to
cause her such distress. The squire had paid
to have things fixed up. The sign had a fresh
coat of paint and we had some new furniture.
He had managed to find a boy to help her, and
when I saw him, it finally hit me what we

were doing. I had not thought about leaving my mother behind and the way of life I had always known. I must admit that I took my mixed feelings out on this poor lad, nagging him more than he really needed it.

The next evening we were on our way. After the squire's changes, the Admiral Benbow did not look as much like my inn and I left it in good spirits. I took a moment to think of the captain, who had been responsible for bringing this all to pass.

We caught the mail coach and I rode squeezed tight beside old Redruth and another heavy man. I had no choice but to sleep and woke up only when we reached Bristol late that evening.

We made our way to an inn down by the harbor, walking along the docks, and seeing all the ships at anchor. I was delighted. Never having been so close to sailing vessels, I was fascinated by the many languages and activities.

I could scarcely believe I was going to sea in a schooner with sailing men who had pigtails and a boatswain who played the pipes. We were sailing for real treasure to an unknown island! This was an adventure other boys could only dream about!

Full of these exciting thoughts, we found Squire Trelawney waiting for us. He was dressed in the bright blue dress of a sailing man, greeting us with a smile as big as my own. We were to sail tomorrow!

The next morning, the squire gave me a note for John Silver and instructions on how to find him at his establishment named the Spy-glass. I was delighted to have the chance to explore on my own and found the whole harbor area full of wonderful sights.

I found the place easily and went inside. It was cheerful and well cared for. The patrons were mostly sailors and the volume of their voices was so high I was almost afraid to enter.

A man with one leg cut off near the hip came out. I was sure this must be Long John Silver. He was able to move around with considerable ease, and he was tall and had a face full of energy and understanding. He moved among his guests, dispensing good cheer to all and sharing jokes with some.

When I had read the squire's letter, I was afraid that the "one-legged man" of the captain and the one in the letter were one and the same. I had dreaded meeting this man. Yet he seemed so good-natured that it was impossible for me to relate him to the filthy Black Dog or the evil blind man, Pew. Reassured, I went inside.

"Are you Mr. Silver?" I asked, and held out the note.

When he saw the note from the squire, he looked at me. Realizing who I was, he held out his hand.

Without warning, one of the patrons sitting near the door jumped up and rushed outside, but not before I had a chance to recognize his face. It was Black Dog! "Stop him!" I yelled.

"Harry, go after him," Silver yelled. "He never paid his bill! Who did you say he was, boy?"

I told him his name was Black Dog, one of the pirates Squire Trelawney had told him about. Soon several others ran after the thief. Long John called a man named Morgan, who had been drinking with Black Dog, to come to him. After talking to Morgan, we were none the wiser. Long John seemed to remember that Black Dog used to come around with a blind man. I told him this must have been Pew, and we both hoped that Long John's men would capture Black Dog.

Silver was jumping up and down and swearing at both men. Seeing Black Dog again had made me wonder about Long John, but his anger convinced me he knew nothing of the two men. Soon his men came back. They told us they had lost Black Dog in the crowded streets and Long John scolded his men for a poor job. At the end of this I was completely convinced of his innocence.

"Hawkins, this be a terrible state of affairs. What will Squire Trelawney think? Here, you find this villain in my place. Now I let 'im get away! For a young lad, you're pretty smart. That's plain to see. You must say a good word in my favor to the squire. When I was younger, I'd a had that villain for sure!" Suddenly, Long John remembered that Black Dog had not paid his bill. He laughed at his memory so hard I could not help but join in.

"I must be getting old! What was I thinking of?" he laughed. "At this rate I'll be no better than ship's boy! Come on, stand by to turn around. A job is a job. I'll grab this old hat, and we'll report t' the squire. Neither one of us got what we wanted out of this event."

As we walked, he told me many things about the harbor and the ships that were docked. He told me what they were carrying and where they were from, amusing me with many stories about seamen he had known. He would make me repeat the nautical terms, patiently teaching me until I began to get them right. I was beginning to look forward to sailing with this unusual man.

Once we reached the squire, Long John repeated the whole episode. I agreed with everything he said. Dr. Livesey and the squire regretted that Black Dog had not been found, but there was nothing more any of us could do. We agreed to reassemble by four o'clock that afternoon for we were to set sail. Long John left us to make his preparations.

Dr. Livesey had not met Long John, and seemed quite impressed with him. The three of us went down to see the *Hispaniola*.

When we finally reached her berth, we were greeted with a salute by Mr. Arrow. He looked very much the pirate with earrings in his ear and a squint to his eye. Mr. Arrow and the squire seemed to get along quite easily, but

I could not help but notice the tension between the squire and Captain Smollett.

The captain seemed to be very displeased with what was on board. Once we had reached the squire's cabin, he asked to meet with us privately. The squire was happy to oblige.

"Sir," said Captain Smollett, "I am not satisfied. I don't like this voyage, I don't like this crew, and I am not happy with my first officer. That just about sums it up for me."

The squire was very upset, asking Captain Smollett if he even liked the ship.

"I don't know yet," he replied. "I haven't seen her under sail, but she seems to be seaworthy." Still not satisfied, the squire asked if the captain liked his employer. Here the doctor interrupted him and asked the captain to explain his position.

"Sir, I was hired on sealed orders with the understanding that I would sail this ship wherever you wanted to go. I can accept that.

"I have found, however, that everybody else seems to know where we are going except me. That does not seem correct to me."

Dr. Livesey agreed with the captain and encouraged him to continue.

"My own crew told me we are going to find treasure. Finding treasure is another matter and can be quite risky. I don't like sailing for treasure, especially when the voyage is supposed to be a big secret. Even Silver's parrot has heard about it. This could be a matter of life or death."

Dr. Livesey agreed with him, but told the captain they were all aware of the risks and still willing to take them. "Why do you dislike the crew so much?" continued the doctor. "Aren't they experienced?" Captain Smollett said he wished he had been allowed to choose the crew himself. Dr. Livesey apologized for not allowing him to have a say in the matter and said the mistake was unintentional.

Captain Smollett continued. "Mr. Arrow in particular may be experienced, but I don't

think the man will respect his authority. He's too friendly with the crew."

"Well, if that's all, tell us what you'd like changed," replied the doctor.

When he was sure they intended to sail anyway, the captain made his requests.

"I don't want the guns and gunpowder up front. I suggest the space under the cabin. I also think the four of you should be berthed together, not separated. Redruth and the boy should occupy the berths beside this cabin." Then he proceeded to shock the squire by telling him of the map and describing the diagrams on it. He also stated the exact longitude and latitude recorded as the location of the treasure.

"What! I gave no one that information!" yelled the squire.

We suspected otherwise, of course, since we knew it had not been us. The doctor and I were certain the squire had been the one responsible. The captain had made his point and requested that neither he, Mr. Arrow, nor any of the rest of the crew know the location and holder of the map.

So it was that the location of the map was to stay a secret and that all of us were to be boarded close together for our own protection.

We would be able to guard the powder and arms on board and, hopefully, prevent a mutiny on the ship. Without these arrangements, the captain would resign.

After the captain left, the squire and the doctor continued to discuss the matter. It was the doctor's opinion that Long John and the captain were honorable men, but the squire still had his doubts about Captain Smollett. I was pleased with the new arrangements for I would be closer to the two men.

Finally the necessary changes were made and the rest of the loading finished. In the afternoon, the crew and Long John came aboard.

He was sent below to prepare the supper and I was dispatched to help him.

CHAPTER 5

The Launch of the Hispaniola

That whole evening was filled with final preparation and farewells from many of the squire's friends. I worked harder than I had ever worked at home at the inn, but found it too exciting to go to bed. Just before sunrise the boatswain started to play his pipes and the crew started to work the capstan-bars. As they pushed the bars, the lines holding the ship started to slacken. Slowly, the current pulled the ship away from the dock. Tired as I was, I stayed to watch us move out of the harbor. As the men worked, Long John broke out into the song I had heard many times from our old captain's lips:

Fifteen men on the dead mate's trunk—
Yo-ho-hum, and a bottle full of rum!

On the "hum" the men would push the bars hard and the ship would move. I could almost hear the old captain singing the words, but in short order, the anchor was up and the sails were unfurled. We were underway and out to sea! I went down to my berth to try to catch some sleep.

The voyage went well and nothing much exciting happened. The *Hispaniola* proved herself well, and the captain was pleased.

Before I tell of the voyage to Treasure Island, certain events need to be told.

In the first place, Mr. Arrow turned out to be worse than the captain had predicted. He was often drunk, although we could not figure out where he got the bottles. The men had no respect for him and simply ignored him. Sometimes he worked; most days he was useless. He was dangerous to himself and we began to fear for his life. Sure enough, one black night, he fell overboard and we saw him no more.

The boatswain, Job Anderson, seemed to be the only man qualified to be promoted to the first mate's job. Squire Trelawney helped by serving a watch or two as well. He had the knowledge and the experience from his previous travels and was good help if the weather was not too rough. If we needed him, the coxswain, Israel Hands, was also quite competent.

Mr. Hands and Long John were close friends. The men called Silver "Barbecue," since he was the cook. Aboard the ship, Long John used a strap around his neck to help carry his crutch, wedging it against the ship as he cooked. With the help of ropes strung around the ship, Long John was able to get around on deck. He sometimes used the ropes and sometimes used his crutch, thus protecting himself against the swaying of the ship. He was as quick as an able-bodied man and quite amazing to watch. "That Barbecue's somethin', that's for sure," said Israel Hands one day. "Been to school right proper. Can talk like a book, if 'es a mind to. He's strong, too, and not a 'feared of anyone. I've seen him fight four men at once and win, unarmed!"

The men admired Silver and everyone respected him and his authority. To me he was always patient and willing to teach. The kitchen was always spotless and his parrot

was kept in a corner in a cage. The parrot, named Captain Flint after the infamous man whose treasure we were now searching, had a way of talking incessantly unless the cover was thrown over the cage.

Long John claimed the bird to be two hundred years old, and he said it had sailed with the great pirate Captain England. In its travels it had been all over the world, picking up phrases from everywhere. Fed sugar from Silver's hand, the parrot would swear as bad as any seaman, which made Long John laugh. The parrot, of course, had no idea what it was saying.

During the voyage, the squire and captain continued to keep their distance from each other, making no secret of their mutual dislike. Captain Smollett was not a talker, never wasting words. If pressed, he might admit he had been wrong about some of the crew, since some performed quite well. We had no complaints about the captain for he did his job very well. He was very pleased with the ship, but said he would reserve final judgement until we had reached home. He still was not happy to be sailing for treasure.

The few times the weather was bad, the *Hispaniola* proved reliable, for which all of us were glad. During the voyage, the squire allowed the crew many liberties, including drink, and the captain was afraid the men would become spoiled. The men were allowed to help themselves to the barrel of apples standing in the middle of the ship, a rare privilege on board a ship. In the end, this was responsible for saving our lives.

As we got closer to Treasure Island, we were running in the trade winds, but I cannot be more specific as to our location. One day, we were close enough to have a lookout posted at all times. We expected to sight land no later than noon the next day. The entire crew was excited.

Just before I turned in for the night, I stopped to get an apple and found the huge barrel almost empty. Nearly everyone was on deck, looking for land. To get to the remaining apples, I had to crawl right into the barrel. The quiet and the gentle rocking must have put me to sleep as I ate the apple, still inside the barrel.

A large man sat down heavily next to the barrel, disturbing my slumber. I was ready to jump up when I heard his voice. It belonged to Long John Silver. As I listened, I was very glad I had not given myself away, for what I heard would later save the lives of the honest men on board.

"No, it wasn't me," he said to someone close by. "I was only quartermaster; Flint was the captain. I lost my leg in the same fight as old Pew lost his eyes. Some master surgeon with lots of schooling cut off me leg, but it didn't save 'im. He 'as hanged and hung out to dry in the sun just like the rest at Corso Castle. Flint's ship was the *Walrus* and it saw plenty of blood and guts, I'll say!"

The youngest deckhand answered back, quite amazed. "I sailed with Captain Flint, but here I am again. I've got nine hundred stashed away. Pretty good for a plain old sailor. Where'd all a' England's finest go, I ask you? Flint's dead. Even Cap'n England's dead. Most of the rest of Flint's crew 'as still left are here on board, most with no money left. Old Pew had lots of money, spent it all. Didn't do him no good anyway, he's dead. Hey, you're pretty smart. I knew when I saw you."

Silver continued to talk to the man, flattering him on how smart he was in the same tone of voice he had used on me. It made me so angry to hear such treachery, I wished I could have killed him myself. Silver planned to come back with his portion of Flint's treasure and become a gentleman for sure, pointing out he had started before the mast, just as the young deckhand now was.

Silver told him his wife had taken all their money and sold their establishment, the Spyglass. She was planning to meet him, but he would not tell the young man where.

Pirates, or "gentlemen of fortune" as they like to call themselves, are not known for trusting each other very much. But Long John was trying to win this man's help and flattered him by insisting he was a trusted comrade. "You see," Silver continued, "I'm different of the rest, if you join yourself with me. Some were afraid of Pew, and some were afraid of Flint. But I tell you, Flint hisself was afraid of me. That crew would've made the devil proud.

They was a rough bunch. If you join with me, you won't have to worry."

The young man seemed convinced and the two shook hands. I wondered how many more of the crew were dishonest. Presently Long John whistled softly and another man joined the two.

I heard the voice of Israel Hands as Hands and Silver discussed Dick, the newest member of their gang. "I want to know, Barbecue, what's going on?" he said. "I'm sick o' Cap'n Smollett, he gits under my skin somethin' fierce. I want to raid his cabin. I'm tired o' watchin' them get all the wine and good stuff."

Silver insulted him and told him he just had to wait. Hands could count on a forward berth and a long life, but only if he followed directions. "You listen here!" Silver said. "When I say the time is right we'll act. Here's Cap'n Smollett, he's a good captain and I'll remind you, he's sailing us to the island and doing a fine job of it. Why should we waste his life and the doctor's while they be doin' all the work. Do you know where the map is? I sure don't. Without it, where would we be? If it's up to me, he can even take us back."

The young man, Dick, protested that all of them were seamen, but Long John reminded them that there was no one qualified to sail the ship. All the men could steer but only Captain Smollett knew how to set the course. He preferred to let Captain Smollett steer them into the main currents before he was to be killed. "You are all the same, too much hurry, an' always wantin' more rum. You all make me sick!" Silver stated. "All those other crews, sure they had their fun, but where they be now? Pew died a beggar. Flint died o' the rum in Savannah. As to what are we gonna do with them? Cap'n England would've left 'em marooned on the island. Flint or Billy Bones would've killed 'em outright."

"I'm just as mean as they are," continued Silver. "A job is a job, and I think they should

all die. I want no evidence turnin' up when I be in Parl'ment as a gentyman! Cut 'em down, I say!"

I was terrified. I was one of the ones they hoped to kill and had no idea how I was to get out of the barrel unnoticed to warn the others. Dick began to go, but I heard Hands stop him, asking for a drink. Silver gave him a key to a cupboard and told him to bring back a drink of rum. Now I knew how the sorry Mr. Arrow had drunk himself to death.

While Dick was absent, Hands and Silver spoke close together and I was unable to hear their conversation. The only thing I could glean was that none of the other men on board would agree to their plan.

Dick returned and several toasts to the plan were drunk. Just as they were finishing, the moon rose full in the sky. In the brightness, someone on deck shouted, "Land, ahoy!"

CHAPTER 6

The Secret Plot
for Treasure Island

Everyone went to look. I took advantage
of the situation and crawled out of the
barrel and joined Hunter and Dr. Livesey
at the front.

The fog had lifted and in the moonlight we
could see some small hills. One was higher
than the others, its top still shrouded in the
mist.

I was still in a state of shock from what I had
heard while in the barrel. Captain Smollett was
directing the men to sail just past the eastern
edge of the island. When all the preparations
were done, the captain turned to the crew and
asked if any of them had been here before.

Silver spoke up and said he had stopped for water once, on another passage. The island was really two islands, the smaller one called Skeleton Island. "It was a pirate island," he explained. "We had a sailor once who knew all 'bout it. The north hill, there, that be Foremast Hill. On the south end are three hills in a row, fore, main, and mizzen. That there big one, the one with all them clouds, that be Spy-glass, 'cus they used to post a lookout there when they stopped to clean their ships, sir."

Captain Smollett told Long John to come have a look at his chart to verify the safest place to drop anchor. Silver found himself looking at a complete copy of the map showing everything except the Xs that marked the treasure and notes about where to find it. Long John was disappointed to find the chart was not the actual treasure map as he had expected, but kept his surprise to himself.

"Here sir," he said. "This here's the spot. This map is very nice. I don't know who could've drawed it so nice; pirates aren't too smart that way. It says here on the map, 'Cap'n Kidd's Anchorage.' That's what that sailor called it. The current runs real strong here to the south, but then it meets another from the west. Use these, and we'll be fine." Captain Smollett thanked him for his help.

I alone knew of Long John's treachery, and I marveled at how well he hid his true experience of the island and his disappointment over the incomplete map. I felt sure it was written all over my face and he would somehow find out I had heard everything. When he touched my arm, I could not help but recoil.

He stopped to chat a moment, telling me how much fun I would have exploring the island and told me to ask him for a snack if I wanted to go ashore. He patted my shoulder and then left me to go below. To my great relief, he had noticed nothing amiss.

I went to where the captain and Dr. Livesey were talking on deck. I tried to get their attention without looking as if I had a big secret to tell. Then Dr. Livesey turned to ask me to fetch some tobacco for his pipe. I took the opportunity to interrupt him and ask him to bring the captain and squire down to the cabin, for I had something terrible to tell them.

The doctor hid his concern very well, concealing our conversation by making a false comment. Turning to the others, they talked briefly and quietly. Soon they were preparing to go down below.

Captain Smollett asked everyone to come on deck and then addressed the crew. He asked the men to raise three cheers for the squire and then the same was given for the captain. All were to have a drink to celebrate and we would go below to toast the health of the crew. "Now boy, I understand you have something you want to tell us," said the squire, when Captain Smollett joined us.

I repeated everything I had heard in the apple barrel. They congratulated me on a job

well done with great courage. Discussing the situation, they concluded that Long John was the ringleader.

"Well, Captain Smollett, I apologize," said the squire. "It seems as if you were correct, after all. I will do whatever you say."

"I am as wrong as you," replied the captain. "I've not seen any sign of this mutiny coming. I should have been more observant. This crew is a puzzle to me."

The doctor and squire asked for the captain's advice. He had several suggestions.

"First, we must keep on going," he said. "Turning back would cause the crew to mutiny for sure. Second, until the treasure is found, we have time to plan and guard ourselves. Third, not all of the crew is dishonest. I'm certain we'll have a fight at some point, but we can make sure it will be at our time, not theirs."

Our goal was still the same. Everyone wanted to find the treasure. We would have to keep our eyes and ears open.

Together we counted seven of us we knew to be honest: Captain Smollett, Dr. Livesey, Squire Trelawney, Hunter, Joyce, Redruth, and myself. When it came to a fight, we would try to strike first and have the element of surprise on our side.

Looking at me, they felt I would be the best candidate to spy on the crew since the men liked me and talked freely in front of me. This was hardly reassuring, but in the end I was the one responsible for our success. At that point we were six men and I, a boy, to the crew's nineteen.

The next morning in the light the whole island was visible. The *Hispaniola* was resting in calm waters off the southeastern coast of the island. From this point we could see the island was covered with forest. The island didn't appear to be a very cheerful place. Yellow sand banks lined the shore and very tall fir trees rose higher than the rest. Rising above the growth were naked hills of rock, very oddly shaped, the tallest of which was Spy-glass. It was three or four hundred feet high and had steep sides and a flat top like a table.

The ship was being banged about by the waves and the constant rocking was making my stomach feel queasy. The dreary appearance of the island and the uneasy threat over us made us fearful instead of relieved at being on land again. I never thought of Treasure

Island with anything but distaste from that time forward.

With no wind, we were going to have to man the small boats and try to row to shore. The sun beat down on us hot and bright, and none of the crew looked forward to the job. Until we spotted land, the men had performed their jobs well, but since then the discipline had fallen to pieces.

Long John was in my boat and he guided us in since, of course, he knew the island so well. We dropped anchor in a spot halfway between the mainland of Treasure Island and the smaller island called Skeleton Island. The trees came right down to the shore and on either side were swamps. The foliage around these areas was a sickly green and did not bode well for our health. We could see nothing of the map's stockade or house, hidden by the trees. If we had not had the map, we would have thought we were the first people on the island. When the doctor looked around he was positive he would be treating cases of malaria and fever.

By now the men's discipline was in tatters. Any order was obeyed with muttering and fierce looks. Even our honest men were in foul moods. I don't know what each expected of Treasure Island but the place did not look like a healthy refuge.

Even Long John could sense the mutiny in the air. He went around encouraging the men, setting a good example by obeying orders at once and with good cheer, singing all the time. The fact that Silver was so concerned worried us even more.

It was the captain's suggestion to allow the men to have the afternoon off on the island. He hoped it would give Long John a chance to talk to the men and quiet them down. We would stay on board ship and thus be able to protect ourselves if they decided to mutiny.

We outfitted ourselves with loaded guns and brought Hunter, Redruth, and Joyce into our confidence. Then the captain assembled all the men on deck. "Men," he said, "you've all earned the afternoon off. Take the small boats and anyone who wants can go exploring. I'll signal with one of the guns before sundown."

Everyone jumped at the chance. Their eagerness, excitement, and good humor returned at once. The cheer they gave echoed over the island, sending the birds to the sky. Silver organized the men while the captain stayed out of sight. It became very obvious that Long John would be their captain if they decided to mutiny.

Our honest men and six others stayed and thirteen rowed for land. At the last minute I decided to go ashore. I knew we six could not defend ourselves as well against the six men left on board, so I slipped into one of the small boats, hidden by the sails.

Only one man noticed and told me to keep my head down. When Silver, who was in a nearby boat, overheard the crewman's comments to me, he asked if I was coming ashore. I started to regret my decision.

We reached the beach, my boat ahead of Silver's. I caught on a branch and headed off into the bush before anyone could stop me, ignoring Silver calling for me through the trees. I ran as fast and far as I could before stopping.

Having satisfied myself that I was far enough away from the others, I looked around. After crossing the swamp, I reached an open plain of sandy soil. In the distance was one of the rugged hills, its rocky sides glistening in the sun.

For the first time in my life I was entirely alone and began to enjoy exploring the area around me. I did not recognize any plants and I often saw snakes sunning themselves on the warm rocks.

I came to an area of dense bush and after that I could see Spy-glass in the distance. Suddenly, an uproar from the wild birds in the

marsh beside me caught my attention. Thinking it must be one of the crew, I caught the sound of a voice coming closer and closer. I quickly hid myself in the thicket. Sure enough, I recognized Silver and someone else. I could not make out what they were saying, but I could tell they were arguing.

When they sat down to talk more quietly, I thought it best to try to eavesdrop. I snuck toward them, crawling on the ground until I reached a hiding place where I could look down on them and hear their conversation.

They were resting in the full sun and Silver was trying to convince the other man to be more patient. "Tom, I put me faith in you, you've got to believe me. You can't give up now! If you change your mind now, I don't know what the others would do to you."

"Silver," said Tom, "I believe you. You're experienced. You're brave. You've saved your coin. How come you're lettin' the rest of them lead you. They're no good." He wasn't buying

Silver's argument. I could tell he was one of the honest men.

Suddenly all of us were taken aback by the sound of another voice, and then a long scream. The multitude of birds were disturbed and rose out of the marsh.

When silence returned, Tom was so startled he stood up. But Silver was sitting still as a mouse watching him very carefully. He knew exactly what had happened. Calmly he told Tom that the scream had belonged to another crewman by the name of Alan, who was killed because he would not go along with Silver's plan.

Tom was terrified and tried to flee, but Silver threw his crutch at him with deadly accuracy and brought him down. I could not tell if he was dead or injured, but I knew his back was broken. Silver very quickly finished him off, stabbing him twice.

CHAPTER 7

Unexpected Company

I fainted. When I came to, Silver was sitting there beside Tom's body, calmly cleaning his knife. It was as if nothing had happened, except I could see the dead man lying on the grass. I had to get away. Already two honest men had lost their lives. What next?

I could hear Silver calling to the other pirates, and I ran as far away from those sounds as I could get. I paid no attention to where I was going but concentrated on putting distance between me and Silver.

What was I to do? I could not appear on the beach when the captain sounded his supper bell and pretend nothing had happened. They

111

would kill me first, and then I would have no chance to tell my friends what had happened. I was sure I would either starve to death or be killed by the pirates. What a choice.

Without knowing, I had come to the two small hills and a densely wooded area, which smelled better and healthier than the marsh. I stopped at once when I saw another strange sight.

I heard the creature first. Its foot disturbed some small stones and turning, I saw it slip behind a tree. I could not tell if it was human or monkey for it seemed to have some sort of fur. This was just as frightening as Silver and his men. Cornered on all sides, I began to think the pirates were a better choice than this unknown threat. I turned and started to flee, watching over my shoulder.

The figure started to cut me off. Tired, I could not compete against something that knew the land. The figure ran like a human on two legs but ran bent over double. It had to be a man. Was it a cannibal?

Again I had to choose. This was definitely human. Maybe I stood a better chance with this creature than with the pirates who were certain to kill me. Suddenly I remembered the loaded pistol in my pocket and began to feel better.

When I stopped running and started to come toward him, the island man became afraid. Finally he came out in the open and threw himself down on his knees, pleading.

"What is your name?" I asked.

"Ben Gunn," he replied. "I haven't talked to anyone for three years. What a poor soul am I."

As I got closer to him, I could see he was not a native but a white man just like me. Against the dark tan of his skin, his light blue eyes were remarkable. His clothes were more ragged than those of the poorest beggar back home. He had made garments from old sails and other canvas. The pieces were fastened together by an odd assortment of buttons, sticks, and things. The only thing I recognized was the belt around his waist.

"What happened to you? Were you ship-wrecked?" I asked.

"No, I was marooned," he said. I had heard of this punishment. A sailor was left on an island by his ship with a little gunpowder and shot and his weapon. "I've been here alone for three years so far," he continued. "I've lived off of goat meat, oysters, and berries. I've not done too badly, I guess. I sure would like something else, though. You don't happen to have some cheese now, do you? I've been dreaming of cheese all this time."

"I'm sorry!" I said. "I don't have anything with me. If I make it back on board, I promise you can have as much as we have."

While we were talking, he looked and felt my jacket, touched my hands, as if genuinely glad to see another human being. When I talked about the difficulty of getting back on board, he gave me a funny look and asked me to explain. Then he asked my name. It seemed to please him.

114

He started to tell me a little about himself. His mother had been very religious, and now he was too, after having been marooned for three years. Looking around, he whispered to me that he was rich.

I was beginning to think he might be senile because he was promising to share his wealth with me. He certainly didn't look rich. Suddenly he asked me if the ship I had come from was Flint's ship.

I had a thought. If he was so afraid of Flint and his men, maybe this unfortunate creature could be trusted after all.

"No, Flint is long dead and most of his crew as well. The rest, unfortunately, are here with us."

"Don't tell me a man with one leg is here!" he gasped.

"It is Silver," I answered, "and he is their captain and our cook."

He was most sorry to hear this and I felt sure now I could trust him with the whole tale. When I was done, he gave my head a pat.

"Good boy, Jim," he said. "You're all in a fix, ain't you? Well you can trust me, Ben Gunn. Now what about your squire? How do you think he'll look on me?"

I assured him the squire was a fair man. I was certain the squire would allow Ben Gunn a share of the treasure, just like the rest of us, if Ben Gunn would help us. What's more, I thought Ben would be allowed to return with us to England, especially since we would be leaving the pirates behind.

He seemed satisfied and told me the rest of his story. He had been with Flint's ship when Flint and six men went ashore and buried the treasure, leaving those on board, including himself, for a week. Flint finally returned in a small boat, alone with his head bandaged and white as a sheet. He told the rest of the crew that the others had died. "None of us could figure how he'd a done it. He said he'd buried 'em all. It was him against the other six, must've been some battle."

He continued his tale. Billy Bones was the first officer, Long John was the quartermaster. When the rest of the crew asked these two where the treasure was, Long John told them they could go ashore and find it if they wanted, but the ship would leave them behind.

Ben Gunn had returned three years ago on a different ship and they had found the island. When he realized where they were, Ben Gunn had told the others about the treasure. "My captain wasn't pleased. The rest of the crew was all for it, so we landed. We spent twelve days lookin' but found nothin'. They got madder and madder at me. Finally we all went back on ship and they gave me a gun, a shovel, and a pickaxe and told me I could stay behind and help myself. Then they left me."

He had seen no one since and had to find what food he could. He hinted that he had

been up to something and I was to tell the squire. I could not understand what he was trying to say and told him so. Besides, I still had not figured out how I was to get back on board to tell the squire anything.

Ben Gunn told me the location of a boat he had made himself. He suggested we might try using it to get me back on board after dark that evening. Without warning, we were startled by the sound of a cannon going off. It was coming from the ship, but it wasn't yet sundown.

I started to run, telling Ben Gunn to come with me. He guided us to the sight of the battle. We could hear another cannon shot and after some time a lot of small arms fire. In front of us we saw a Union Jack flag flying on a pole.

CHAPTER 8

The Doctor's Tale

It is now I, Dr. Livesey, who can tell the tale of those left on board. About one-thirty in the afternoon, or three bells in shipping terms, the captain, the squire, and I were discussing our plans in the cabin. If there had been enough breeze to sail, we would have killed the six men left behind and set sail for home. We could not sail without the wind, and Hunter had come to tell us that young Jim Hawkins, one of our party, had slipped ashore with the rest of the pirates.

We did not think for a moment that he had switched sides, but we were concerned for his well-being. We knew the pirates to be in an evil mood and we were afraid of what they would do to young Jim.

We went up on deck where our nostrils were filled with the awful smell of the swamp. The heat caused the pitch to ooze in the seams of the ship and I was sure all of us would be afflicted with fever and dysentery.

The six crewmen who had stayed on board were sitting on deck scowling, while on shore each of the boats was guarded by a pirate.

After some difficult waiting, we decided that Hunter and myself should use the jolly-boat to get ashore to see what was happening. Hunter and I steered past the pirates' landing site, causing the pirate guards to rise and try to decide what to do about us. If they had run off to tell Silver, things might have turned out differently, but they stayed and went back to their whistling.

We moved on around the coast and out of sight of the two guards. Hunter and I landed quite close to the stockade with our guns ready to fire.

We found the log house, sitting on top of a spring of clear, safe water, and the stockade, which was large enough to hold forty people easily. It was designed to be protected by musket holes around the walls. The house was built in a clearing and surrounded by a strong, six-foot-tall wall built around the perimeter. Those inside would be safe from intruders—they would have a clear view of anyone running from the bush. As long as the occupants had enough food to eat and were able to set up a watch, they would have the advantage.

I was especially happy to see the spring because I knew the water near the swamp was not fit to drink. The one thing we had lacked on the *Hispaniola* was fresh water. While trying to decide what to do, we heard the scream of a man dying. I wrongly assumed Jim Hawkins had been killed.

Even though I have served as a soldier, I am a doctor first. Hunter and I returned at once to our boat and were soon back on board the ship.

Everyone was fine, although shocked at the thought of this death. "There is another one of their six who is pretty scared," said the captain. "If anything else happens, I think he'd come over to join us."

We talked quickly of my plan and then Redruth was installed in the area between the cabin and forecastle. We gave him several loaded guns and a mattress for protection. Hunter, Joyce, and I started to load the boat full of provisions to take to the stockade. We loaded gunpowder, guns, biscuits, casks of pork, a keg of cognac, and my medicine chest.

While we were at work, the squire and captain remained on deck. With loaded guns, they confronted the six remaining crew members telling them that if they even moved, they would be killed. One of these men was Israel

Hands. After looking at each other, they turned and fled toward the rear. Here they encountered Redruth and then thought better of trying to attack us. They hid on deck and bothered us no more for quite a while.

With the jolly-boat loaded as full as we dared, Hunter, Joyce, and I set off for the stockade. The guards watched us as before and this time, one went in search of his comrades on shore. I was tempted to destroy their boats, but I let them be since I did not know how far away the others were.

The three of us carried everything we could to the stockade. Hunter and I left Joyce—with several loaded guns—to protect the stockade while we returned to unload the rest of the provisions from the jolly-boat. When everything was safely stored, I left Joyce and Hunter on shore and returned to the ship.

We wanted to take another load to the stockade even though it was only a matter of time before we were discovered. We dropped whatever powder and arms we could not carry into the sea. We set off again with the squire, captain, and Redruth coming with me this time. Captain Smollett shouted to the men left on board. "Abraham Gray, I want to talk to you."

He got no answer.

"Gray," he repeated, "I am still your captain, and I am ordering you to come with me. You are a good man, I'll give you thirty seconds to come."

Silence.

"Men, every second you hesitate risks the lives of the rest of these good men."

A minute later, we heard the sounds of a fight. Abraham Gray came running out, his cheek bleeding from a cut.

"I'm coming with you, sir," he said.

He was the man the captain hoped would join us.

This had to be our final trip because the little boat was terribly overloaded with men and

provisions. With the captain's help we made better progress, but we were risking our lives to be on the open water. With the tide out and the currents changing, I was not sure we would even make it to the stockade. I was afraid we would end up where the pirates had landed.

"What about the gun?" said the captain, concerned. I spoke up.

"I don't think we have to worry, sir. They will never be able to move it off the ship and through the trees."

The captain directed our sight to the larger cannon on the rear of the ship. To our horror, we saw the pirates left behind on the ship getting ready to load and fire at us. I realized with dismay that the cannon's ammunition had not been dumped and it would take them little time to find it.

"Israel Hands was the gunner on Flint's ship," said Abraham Gray.

We were heading straight for the beach in front of the stockade, but this left us directly in the line of fire from the cannon. Hands was working furiously to load the gun.

We decided that Squire Trelawney, our best shot, would try to kill the men on board, preferably Hands. When he was ready, he fired. The most exposed on board, Hands still managed to miss being hit by the squire's shot but one of the other men was hit. He gave a loud cry and we heard it echo on shore.

Then we saw the other pirates coming out of the woods and boarding the boats. We rowed as hard as we could, not caring whether we swamped the boat, for we were as good as dead out on the water.

We made good progress and headed around the coast so that the little boats could no longer see us. The ship's cannon was still a threat and the squire tried firing at the ship again. Someone else on board the ship was hit. It was the cannon fire that Jim Hawkins heard, although we would not know that for quite a while.

We were not hit directly but our boat sank in the three feet of water very close to the stockade. This was terrible, for our provisions went with it. Only two of the five guns were saved.

We could hear the pirates coming through the woods and knew that if we wanted to live we had to make it to the safety of the stockade. We just hoped that Hunter and Joyce would help us and ran as fast as we could to safety.

I asked the captain to pass his gun to the squire, since his gun had gotten wet and was useless. I gave Gray my cutlass since he had nothing. I could tell by the way he swung the blade that we would be able to rely on him.

Just as we reached the outside of the stockade, seven of the pirates appeared. They stopped for a moment, surprised to see us, and we had the chance to fire the first shots. One was hit and the rest turned and headed back into the bush.

Once inside the shelter we had a moment to be grateful—but only that. A shot whizzed by our heads and hit Tom Redruth. We tried to return fire, but the pirates were already gone. I turned my attention to Tom and could see he was hurt pretty badly.

This man had come with us on our adventure without complaining once and had been a stalwart help. He had followed every order, never questioning. He was the oldest of our party, and now his time was over. In tears, the squire held his hand, and poor Tom asked me if he was going to die. I had to tell him he was. After we read a prayer at his request, he died quietly.

The captain produced one Union Jack flag and hung it from the roof. He placed another one over Tom's body. After some comforting words to the squire, he turned to me. "When is the other ship expected?" he asked.

I told him it would not set sail for several months. He was not too pleased. He then proceeded to inventory our provisions.

"That puts us in a tight spot," he said. "We lost a lot of food when our boat sunk. We have enough gunpowder and shot, but our food will be very short. With those pirates outside we won't be able to hunt or fish." Pointing to Redruth's body, he said it was a help to have one less mouth to feed.

Suddenly another round of shots passed overhead and into the woods. The captain hoped the pirates would just keep on shoot-

ing, wasting what little powder they had, and thereby giving us the advantage.

They were trying to hit the flag, and we decided not to take it down in spite of their efforts. The pirates kept up the barrage all evening, but hit nothing of any importance.

In our haste to get inside, we had left some of our supplies outside the stockade, on the opposite side of where the shooting was coming from. When Gray and Hunter tried to bring the supplies inside, they found the pirates had already helped themselves. Now each pirate was armed with musket and shot.

The captain made the entry in his log:

Alexander Smollett, captain: David Livesey, physician; Abraham Gray, carpenter's hand; John Trelawney, proprietor of ship; Richard Joyce and John Hunter, servants—these are the loyal men left of the ship's party—landed today on Treasure Island with enough

*food for ten days on spare rations. We
flew the British colors above the roof.
Tom Redruth, owner's servant, shot by
mutineers from ship. Jim Hawkins,
cabin-boy—"*

Just as the captain was about to write and I
was wondering myself what had happened to
Jim myself, I heard someone calling us on the
land side.

When we went to investigate, we found
young Jim Hawkins climbing over the stockade wall in fair health.

CHAPTER 9

Jim Returns

Now I, Jim Hawkins, will resume the tale. When Ben Gunn, who had been running with me, saw the English flag above the stockade, he made me stop. "That's got to be your friends," he said.

"It's probably Silver and his gang," I replied.

"Nay, mate! Pirates would be flying the Jolly Roger, never the ensign of 'is majesty. That's Flint's old stockade. He sure was somethin'. Rum was th' only thing that got the best of 'im. Only one he was afraid of was gentleman Silver."

I was all the more eager to go to my friends, but Ben cautioned me to wait. He would go no further until he had the squire's word that he would be accepted. "You know where you can find me," he said. "But what man tries to find me, has to carry somethin' white in 'is hand. He also has to say:'Ben Gunn has his own reasons.' I had no idea what he had been trying to hint at."

"I suppose I understand," I told him. "You have something the squire or doctor should hear, but we have to come to you. Is that it?"

He seemed satisfied and agreed to wait from noon to six o'clock that evening. Then I was allowed to go, but only after I gave him my assurances that I would not turn him over to Silver. He hinted that if the mutineers were to camp on the island for the night, there would be fewer of them in the morning.

We stopped talking when a cannon ball came flying past our spot. We quickly separated as we ran for cover. The gunfire was intense, so I kept moving from spot to spot. I finally began to see a pattern in the firing and detoured around to the east of the stockade.

It was sunset and the air was turning chilly. I was glad I still had my jacket. I could see the *Hispaniola* still anchored where we had left her, but above the mast flew the Jolly Roger. After one last shot was fired from the ship, all was silent.

I watched the pirates carrying some of the boxes of provisions away into the woods and could see a huge bonfire off in the distance.

Some were singing. It was obvious they had found some rum.

After a while, I was pretty sure I could try for the stockade. As I made my way along the coast, I could see a very high, white rock sitting by itself on the spit of sand connecting the two islands. This might be the rock where Ben Gunn kept his boat, and I hoped to have the opportunity to look another time. I continued to make my way until I was able to reach the stockade from the landward side. I climbed in and was relieved to be greeted warmly by my friends.

I told my tale and then had the opportunity to look around. The house was entirely built of logs and raised off the ground about a foot and a half. The spring was located under the porch and pooled into an old iron kettle, probably one from Flint's ship. An old hearth was all that was left inside the house.

Flint's men had cleared the inside of the stockade using trees to build the house. It would have been a lovely grove of trees before they destroyed it. Only sand was left now, the soil washed away, leaving only a little patch of moss and ferns next to the spring.

Surrounding the stockade, the trees took over again. Fir trees lay inland and oaks on the sea side.

The evening wind crept through every hole in the walls, bringing with it a continual dusting of sand to get into our hair, eyes, clothes, and stores. Even our food tasted like sand. Our tea fairly boiled with the stuff, causing our eyes to water and our throats to burn.

I saw Abraham Gray's cheek was cut and bandaged and poor old Tom Redruth lay dead on the floor under the flag.

It would have been easy for us to give way to despair. However Captain Smollett never let us escape into melancholy. We were divided up to do shifts of watches and I was partnered with Gray and Dr. Livesey. Even though we were tired, there was plenty of work to be done. Two fetched firewood, and two built a grave for Redruth. The doctor was appointed cook, and I was the door sentry. The captain worked as hard as we did, pitching in wherever needed.

The doctor went to cook inside. The only chimney was a hole in the roof, so he came out from time to time to escape the continual smoke. He watched the captain, commenting to me on what a fine man he was. He asked me about Ben Gunn. We discussed whether the man had gone insane while living all alone on the island. The doctor revealed that he had in his possession a large piece of Parmesan cheese, and he was willing to offer it to Ben Gunn in reward for his help.

Tom Redruth was buried after supper, and then the three in authority sat down to make plans. They figured our best plan was to try to kill the pirates until they either gave up or tried to sail away. We knew that there were no more than fifteen left, with at least two injured. If we could use every opportunity to reduce their numbers while preserving our own, we were fairly sure we would win. We had two other factors in our favor: rum and the climate.

We could hear them drunk half a mile away. Since they were camped in the marsh, the doctor was sure there would be several cases of fever very shortly.

Finally I was able to sleep and woke up after the rest had eaten their breakfast. When they shouted that Long John was coming toward the stockade with the white flag of truce, I jumped up to watch from a hole in the wall.

Silver and another man were standing out-side, surrounded by fog still lifting from the ground. The captain ordered us indoors, fear-ing a plot to trick us. He stood sheltered by the porch in case he was fired upon and hailed Silver from the distance. When he heard Silver wanted to talk, he directed us to stand watch with loaded guns around the walls.

"What are we to do with your flag of truce?" asked the captain.

"Cap'n Silver would like to talk, sir!" was the reply.

"I never heard of him!" yelled the captain, muttering under his breath about Silver's promotion.

"The boys chose me to be cap'n, sir," Silver replied, "after you deserted the ship." Silver stressed the word "deserted."

"We're here to call a truce if we can agree. If you give me your word, Cap'n, that I'll be safe inside and allowed to git away after we talk, I'll come inside."

The man with Silver tried to dissuade him, but Silver came ahead advancing alone. He climbed the stockade wall, crutch and all. I admit that if we had been attacked, I would have proved a useless sentry. I was too interested in what was going on before me. The captain was waiting for Silver down by the spring. He watched as Long John made slow progress across the inside clearing through

the sand. He was dressed in his best, a great huge blue coat with shiny brass buttons.

The captain told him to sit down, although Silver would have preferred to go inside. The captain offered him no choice.

"If you would have done what you were hired to do, Silver, you would still be sitting in your warm galley. You were treated well then. Are you still my ship's cook, or Cap'n Silver, the pirate thief? If it's the captain, then you'll hang for sure."

Silver looked around and greeted us all warmly. Then he noticed me, but only greeted me with friendliness. The captain told him to get on with it.

"You're right again, sir. A job is a job. That was a good fight last night. Some of my men was shook up for sure, and even me a bit. I'm here to make a deal. We'd best ease up a bit o' the rum, for I's the on'y one sober last night. I's just tired. If I hadn't been so tired, I would have seen you do it. Now he's dead and we've lost 'im."

The captain told him to continue, never betraying the fact that he did not have a clue what Silver was talking about. I did, though. I remembered Ben Gunn's threat to make widows of several of the crew. I figured he had been up to some good mischief while the pirates were drunk and sleeping. Now there were only fourteen!

Silver continued. "We still want the treasure," he said. "You be wantin' your lives, and I'm sure we can come t' terms if you swap us the map."

Captain Smollett was not buying this deal at all, knowing Silver's men would kill us anyway. Silver threatened Gray, but the captain said Gray had told us nothing. Captain Smollett threatened to blow Silver, his men, and the island away before he'd settle on those terms.

The two men sat and smoked their pipes for a while before continuing. Silver went on. In return for the chart, and if we would stop killing his men, he promised on his word to put us

ashore somewhere safe once the treasure was loaded into the ship. Otherwise, he offered to divide up the treasure fairly, and he would tell the first ship he saw to pick us up. He thought he was being very generous, and told all of us, in a loud voice, that the deal he struck with the captain would be offered to each of us.

Captain Smollett simply stood up, shook out his pipe, and asked if that was everything.

Long John told him that was it, or we'd see only musket balls from now on. It was now the captain's turn.

"Now you listen to me. If each of you comes back, unarmed, I will have you placed in leg irons. I will gladly take you home to England to stand trial for mutiny, and I promise as the English captain, Alexander Smollett! You can't win. You don't know where the treasure is, and not one of you can sail the ship. You aren't even good fighters, for Gray managed to escape from five of you. Master Silver, not 'Captain' Silver, you are finished! This is the last time I'll speak to you fairly. I intend to take you back to England to pay for your crimes, or I'll see you dead first. You may leave at once!"

Of course, this did not set well with Silver. I thought his eyes would pop out of his head.

"Someone help me up!" he cried. No one did and so the man was forced to crawl to the porch and get himself upright. He spat into our fresh spring water in hatred. Then, threatening to destroy us all within the hour, he slowly made his way to the wall and crawled over, disappearing into the woods.

When he had seen the last of Silver, the captain turned around. He found all of us, except Gray, staring after the pirate and not minding our sentry positions at all. We justly deserved his anger. Gray's name was to be added to the log, but the rest of us wore very red faces. After a moment, he continued.

"Gentlemen, I just fired the first shot at Silver and surprised him. I did it intentionally, and I fully expect we will be attacked within the hour. While they have more men, we have shelter and, until a moment ago, I thought we had more discipline. Now I have my doubts. I am sure we can win the fight if we want to."

He went around the stockade, checked our defenses, and was pleased. Each of us had several muskets and a pile of ammunition. In the center of the clearing were the cutlasses. He gave instructions to put out the fire. I was told to get something for breakfast and resume my post as soon as possible. When all was ready he gave us our orders.

"Dr. Livesey, you are to guard the door. Don't show yourself; stay tucked inside, and shoot through the porch. Joyce, you stand on the west corner. Squire Trelawney, since you are our best marksman, I want you and Gray to man the long north wall. There are five musketholes there, and I'm sure we can expect the fight to come from that side. We must not let them get to the walls. Then they could fire at us through the holes and we would have little protection.

Hawkins, since you and I are not very good at shooting, we will stand by to help the rest."

The sun was now high in the sky and soon the very sand had reached a boiling point. The anxiety of waiting had us at a similar boiling point. It was a long, hot hour before anything happened. Joyce wanted permission to fire at anyone he saw and the captain gave it. Still we waited.

Each of us was straining our eyes to see, when suddenly Joyce took aim and fired. Shots rang out from every side of the stockade for a few minutes and then all was silent. Joyce was disappointed he had hit no one, and we tried to count how many men they had by the location of the shots they had fired. From our calculations we figured the attack would come from the north and the other sides would only be harassed. Captain Smollett wanted us to remain where we were.

A loud yell was heard as some of the pirates burst out of the woods from the north, running straight for the stockade. A rifle-ball came flying in from the same location. The doctor's musket was destroyed.

The invaders clambered over the fence, but not before the squire and Gray were able to hit three, although one was able to turn and scoot back into the woods. Four were now inside the stockade. Several more kept up a steady barrage of fire from the woods. In a moment the four were on us.

The first to appear was Job Anderson, the ship's boatswain. Another grabbed Hunter's gun and pulled it from his hands, managing to knock him senseless on the floor. The third fell on the doctor, who was armed with only his cutlass.

Now they had the advantage and we had lost it. Many shots had been fired at the log-house, filling it with smoke, but the captain ordered us inside. Utter chaos reigned. We could hear many cries and see the flashes from the firing guns. I heard one loud groan close beside me. The captain ordered us out.

With cutlasses in hand, we resumed the fight outside. Someone cut my hand, but not badly. I saw the doctor finish one man off, knocking him down the porch stairs and slashing his face. When the captain ordered us to go behind the house, I noted a change in his voice.

We all obeyed and in a flash I came face to face with Anderson. He held his cutlass high to cut me down, but I managed to jump aside and roll down the hill.

I saw a pirate wearing a red nightcap crawling over the fence, his cutlass wedged between his teeth. Another was hot on his heels, but in the space of time it took me to stand up, the battle was over and we had won.

Gray had been right behind me and had finished off one. Another pirate lay dying in great pain, his gun still in his hand.

The third had been killed by the doctor. The fourth to come across, Mr. Red-Cap, had dropped his cutlass on the ground and was now desperately trying to get back across. He made it, and vanished into the woods with the rest. Altogether five of their men died, but we did not have a moment to lose.

We took shelter in the house only to find that Hunter lay unconscious, Joyce dead, and the captain injured. We were now four to nine, although we found out much later that another one of their men had died. Our odds seemed to be improving.

155

CHAPTER 10

The Start of My Sea Adventure

Contrary to our expectations, the pirates did not come back. We were able to have some dinner and attend to our wounded. Despite the risk, the squire and I cooked outside, trying not to listen to the groans coming from the house as the doctor did his work.

Hunter never regained consciousness and one of the pirates died as the doctor tried to help him. The captain would recover. His shoulder blade was broken and Dr. Livesey was worried it might puncture his lung. He had also suffered a wound to his leg. He was under

157

strict instructions from the doctor to keep his arm still and speak as little as possible.

The doctor bandaged the cut on my hand and after dinner, he and the squire started talking. Sometime after noon, the doctor strapped on a cutlass, put the treasure map into his pocket, hoisted a gun, and left.

Gray and I had not participated in their conversation and we were therefore speechless at the doctor's actions. I assured him the doctor had not taken leave of his senses. I was pretty sure he was heading off to find Ben Gunn. My guess was correct, although it would be some time before we knew for sure.

The sun was now beating over our heads, and the open stockade and hot log house offered us no protection from the heat. I began to wish I could disappear into the woods as well, which was not a very smart idea at all. The heat, the smell of blood, and the knowledge that I was surrounded by dead men began to fill me with disgust.

I was supposed to be washing things up from the fight and our dinner, but as I got closer to the bag our bread was stored in, a plan started to take shape in my mind. I loaded my pockets with biscuits.

What I did was very stupid, but I had absolutely made up my mind. The biscuits would keep my hunger at bay, at least until tomorrow. I took a couple of pistols and still had the rest of my powder and bullets from the battle. I felt I was well prepared.

It was my intention to go to the white rock I had seen before, hoping to find Ben Gunn's small boat. Since I was sure no one would allow me to go, I was going to have to slip away unnoticed. Here I made my first mistake.

I managed to crawl out and reach the trees before anyone could stop me. My second mistake was to leave two men to guard the stockade. Luckily, everything worked out for the best.

It was cooler in the trees, and from the sound of the surf, I could tell the winds off the

sea were high. Not too long after, I reached the beach and watched the rolling waves beat upon the rocks from a spit of land jutting out into the sea.

I made my way to some bushes in front of where the *Hispaniola* lay anchored. The wind had now died and fog was moving in. I had a clear view of the ship, though, and could see the pirate flag flying from its mast.

Beside the ship was one of the small boats, and I recognized Silver and Mr. Red-cap laughing at some joke. Suddenly I heard a frightening scream. I soon realized the sound came from Silver's parrot, Captain Flint, sitting on his shoulder.

The sun was setting fast and I knew I had work to do if I hoped to find Ben Gunn's boat before dark. It took quite a while to make my way down the spit to the white rock and when I reached it, it was almost night. I found a small pit below the rock with a little covering of goatskins.

I lifted off the skins to find a very rough contraption. This vessel was made of wood and covered with goatskin, the hair on the inside of the boat. It was lopsided and very small and I could not understand how Ben Gunn could fit inside, much less make it move. A thwart was placed very low in the bottom for seating and a double paddle aided in steering.

Many years later I heard about the coracle boats that native people make. This vessel resembled the primitive lightweight boats made from animal hides and saplings or reeds for the frame. Very small, they skim over the surface of the water. This was certainly a very rough one. Its great advantage was its light weight.

Having found the boat, I should have returned to the stockade. But I did not. I decided to paddle out to the *Hispaniola* under cover of darkness and cut her adrift. Then she would float away and the pirates would have no further advantage from her. Since the pirates had taken the small gigs with them and left the *Hispaniola* by itself, I thought there would be little risk of getting caught.

I sat down to eat and wait for total darkness. The fog was now thick and I could see only two things. The pirates had lit another huge bonfire on shore and I could hear them drinking again in the swamp. In the water, I could see some light from the ship. The tide had swung her around so that her bow was now facing me. The cabin lights were lit and would have to guide my way.

After wading through some shallow water, I came to the sea and set my little boat on the surface. She proved to be safe to use, but it took me forever to figure out how she worked. No matter what I tried, she would move in the direction opposite the wind, bringing me back to the shore. I spent a lot of time going around and around in circles.

I am sure that I would never have reached the ship without the help of the tide. The coracle I was in was so small and the ship so large, I could hardly miss her. I managed to make it to the hawser, the rope holding the anchor. I grabbed it.

The tide was strong and I knew if I cut the hawser, the *Hispaniola* would soon be carried away. But then I remembered that the cut string would snap out of control like a knife once the tension was gone. It would probably knock me and my little craft into the sea.

I did not know what to do. At that moment the wind blew the *Hispaniola* toward her anchor, slackening the tension on the hawser. I took out my gully knife and cut until it was held by two strands. Then I had to wait for another puff of wind.

I could hear voices from the cabin and I recognized them as those of Israel Hands and Mr. Red-cap. Hands was the man who had fired at us from the ship. When he had sailed with captain Flint, he had been Flint's gunner. Both men were drunk and were pitching their empty bottles out the cabin windows into the sea. I could hear the sound of a furious argument but nothing more ever happened.

I could also hear the drunken pirates on shore, singing old sailor songs. They were as callous as the words they sang.

Only one man of her crew still alive,
On a ship that sailed with seventy-five.

The breeze freshened once more and with another cut from my knife, the *Hispaniola*

was free. The ship began to turn and move in the current, and I was in serious danger of being knocked out of the coracle. Just as I finally managed to shove myself free, my hands felt a narrow rope that was hanging down from above. By instinct, I grabbed it at once and held on for dear life.

I barely had time to form the idea in my head. Hand over hand, I crawled up the rope, hoping to look into the window. The ship and coracle now in the current, were drifting fairly fast, and we had moved alongside the bonfire. As I looked in the window, I could tell the two inside had not noticed the signs that the ship was moving. They were fighting, each trying to strangle the other.

I dropped down again into the coracle and let my eyes grow accustomed to the darkness. I could hear the pirates singing on shore, going on about the devils of drink. Drink was probably also the cause of the problem inside the ship. Suddenly the coracle moved and the ship changed course. Both were moving south, heading for the open sea. We had passed right by the drunken pirates at their campfire, but they never even noticed.

As she pitched and changed directions, the two inside the ship finally came to their senses. I lay down in the bottom of the coracle, sure I would be dashed to pieces on the rocks. Amazingly, I finally fell asleep, dreaming of home and the old inn.

I awoke in the morning to find myself at the southwest end of Treasure Island. I could not see the sun as it was blocked by the height of Spy-glass in front of me.

To the side were Haulbowline Head and Mizzen-mast Hill, and I should have turned and paddled for shore. However, I would not have been able to land on shore since this part of the shoreline was full of rocks and the waves would have finished me off for sure. In front of me on the rocks were creatures that looked

167

like huge slimy snails. The sight of them was so disgusting I was ready to risk starving to death first. Only much later would I find out they were simply sea lions.

Silver had talked about this part of the island and I tried to remember what he had said about the current that runs alongside.

To my amazement, I was able to make my way with the coracle. After many attempts, I found the best progress was made when I lay in the bottom. When I tried to paddle, she would threaten to swamp or pitch me overboard, terrifying me.

After a while, I regained my courage and peeked above the gunwale to watch her move. I also tried sitting up and paddling a bit. I soon found that by staying low in the boat to keep her balanced and occasionally paddling toward the island, I could make headway. The only drawback was that the position in which I had to lay was very awkward and tiring. The coracle had her own way of running the waves, and I came to the conclusion, I must let her lead me. The waves resembled the hills and valleys found on land. The little coracle found her own way through the valleys and avoided the watery hillside slopes.

I found by occasionally paddling at the side, I pushed us farther to land. It was pretty sure I would make it close to Cape of the Woods.

My biggest problem now was thirst. The sun beat down on me and I was not able to land where I wanted because I was too far out in the current. Almost sick with dismay, I looked up and saw in front of me the ship.

I no longer cared if those on board saw me. I truly needed some water. The main sail and two jibs were up and she was heading for the northwest. Thinking Hands and Mr. Redcap were circling the island, I was surprised to find she changed course and was heading due west. Then she stopped, helpless in the wind's eye. She continued in this fashion for a few more minutes, sliding one way and then the other. It was only then that I realized no one was steering her. Either they had deserted her or were too drunk to do anything.

What if I could get on board and steer her toward the stockade? With a great deal of determination and hard work, I made my way to the boat, sometimes having to stop and bail out my little craft. I soon figured out how to guide the coracle and gradually worked my way toward the ship.

It was going to be very hard to catch her, not because she was moving very fast but because she would start and then stop dead still.

Finally I had my opportunity, although she turned around and nearly crashed right over top of me. I had to stand in the coracle and push it down out of the ship's way, catching the jib-boom with my hands and bracing my feet against the ship to get on board. Clinging for dear life, I heard the coracle break up under the ship. Now I was stuck on board for sure.

CHAPTER 11

Captain Hawkins

The ship jerked the other way and I nearly fell off. I fell on deck on the lee-side of the forecastle but could see no one. As the ship turned again and the mainsail swung around, I could make out her two watchmen.

Mr. Red-cap was dead, stretched out on the deck. Israel Hands lay propped against the bulwarks, his face as white as a sheet. As the ship continued to pitch and roll, Mr. Red-cap followed. Hands seemed to be mortally injured and ready to join his mate. As he rolled closer to me, I could see the deck was covered in blood.

173

At a calm moment, he rolled on his side and started to groan. With great difficulty, he propped himself upright again. I started to feel pity for him until I remembered the conversation I overheard in the apple barrel.

I walked over to him, jokingly inviting him on board. I could make out only one word: brandy. When I went to fetch it, I found the cabin and lower deck in an awful state. The place was filthy and had been trashed, but I found a bottle in the cellar and took it up to him. I also found some food for myself and finally got a good drink of water.

After he had had his fill of brandy, I asked him how badly hurt he was. He couldn't tell me, but asked me how I had gotten on board.

"I'm here to take over this ship and return it to Captain Smollett," I replied. "Until further notice, I am the new captain, and I want you to treat me as such."

He merely grunted but made no move to stop me. The brandy had restored his color but that was all. He was still a very sick man. I told him I was going to remove the Jolly Roger and threw it overboard. All this time he simply watched me, a very sly look on his face.

"Now Cap'n Hawkins, I s'pose you'll be wantin' to go ashore. How 'bout we have us a little talk?"

I agreed and continued to eat my meal with relish. "That," he said looking at the dead man, "was O'Brien. We rigged the sails, hopin' to sail her back. Now's he's dead. I don't know who'll sail this here ship. You be too small; it's a man's job, that's for sure. If'n you give me some grub and more of that brandy and bandage my wound, I could tell you what to do. Maybe's you could sail her. That's all I's can think of."

"I'm not going back to our landing spot," I told him. "I want to beach the ship in North Inlet." He agreed, having little choice, and the deal was made. It wasn't long before we were underway and making excellent progress. With the aid of a handkerchief, Hands was able to bind up his great thigh wound and then eat a little food. He was beginning to look a little better and his instructions were sounding clearer.

There was a nice, stiff breeze to sail by, and I was beginning to feel a little less guilty for deserting my companions. The one thing that kept up my guard was the smile on Israel Hands' face. It was a smile both old and weak, but still dangerous as he slyly watched my every move.

Aided by the wind, we made our way to the North Inlet, but we could only wait until the tide had gone before we could beach her. He told me how to lay the ship to and it took me several attempts before I succeeded. We ate our dinner in silence.

"Cap'n Hawkins, would you consider tossin' the body of my dead mate, O'Brien, overboard? I don't relish lookin' at him."

I did not think I was strong enough to do the job and said I was content to leave him.

We talked for a while and he asked for a bottle of wine, saying the brandy was too strong.

I did not believe him for a moment. He really wanted me to leave him alone. I could tell by the expression on his face that he had a plan up his sleeve. I decided to play along with his notion and told him I would be a few minutes.

With as much noise as possible, I descended the companion-way and then crept silently back up again, keeping out of sight. I saw him rise to his hands and knees, groaning all the while, and crawl across the deck. In a coil of rope, he found a knife concealed there. Picking it up, he hid it in his jacket, not even caring that it was covered in blood. He gingerly made his way back to where he had been sitting before.

I had a problem. Mr. Hands was mobile and armed and I was to be his next victim. I did not know when he planned to kill me. What I did know was that both of us wanted the ship safe, beached someplace where one of us could retrieve her and sail out of this wretched place. I was sure I would be allowed to live until then.

I brought up the bottle of wine and found him just as I had left him, although he was trying to look a little weaker. After a few minutes, he started to tell me about himself.

"I've been sailing close on thirty years," he said seriously. "I've seen all kinds of weather, fair and foul. I've been on ships where food was scarce, fights goin' on, everything. From my recollectin', being good does you no good. He 'as strikes first al'ays wins. Dead men don't talk, that's my way o' seein' things."

Suddenly his tone altered. The tide had changed and he started to give me instructions again.

The course was difficult, and Hands did an excellent job of telling me what to do. We managed to avoid the shoals and rocks as if we had done this a million times.

As we cleared the headland, the island closed in around us. The water we were in was more of an estuary or river, long and narrow.

We could see in front of us the remains of an old ship, rotting where she lay. It was a depressing sight, so overgrown with seaweed and bushes, but it showed the water was calm.

Hands pointed out a spot to beach the *Hispaniola*. It was full of smooth sand and surrounded by trees. He told me it would be

feasible to float the ship again with the help of the incoming tide and several men pulling it out with ropes. With careful instructions he told me what to do and soon the ship was beached just as he had ordered.

I had been so busy obeying his commands that I had not kept watch. Out of the corner of my eye, or maybe from instinct, I saw him coming at me with the knife outstretched in his hand.

My yell was full of fright, but his was one of anger. As he rushed forward, I dodged to the side and grabbed the tiller. This caused it to turn and hit him in the chest, stunning him for a moment.

I took the chance to get out of the corner and run. Turning around, I drew my pistol, aimed, and pulled back the trigger. It did nothing, useless from getting wet with sea water. Swearing, I was beginning to despair, amazed at how fast such a badly injured man could move.

I could not back up for he would merely corner me at the stern. I planted myself against the main mast and waited, hidden by its size. He paused for he could tell I meant to dodge the other way, and we danced back and forth as I had done as a child playing tag. This time it was in earnest and my life was on the line.

Suddenly the ship pitched in the sand on her side at an angle, and both of us rolled into the scuppers, almost on top of each other.

My head and his feet hit with enough force to make my teeth rattle. Hands had the worst of it, though; he had gotten mixed up with O'Brien's stiff body. I leaped up into the mizzen sails and crawled up to the crosstrees.

He had been quick to respond but not quick enough. He sat below with his mouth open in shock, too injured to climb. I took the time to fix the priming of my pistol and loaded the other one for good measure.

Hands began to see that things were starting to go against him, and he attempted to climb himself. I could hear him groaning and before he was too far up, I was ready.

"Come any further, Mr. Hands, and I'll shoot! Dead men don't talk, as I'm sure you've heard!"

He did stop and removed the knife from his mouth so he could talk. We had reached a stalemate. He proposed that we should talk.

Smiling full of bravado, I was still thinking about his words, when his right hand went back over his shoulder. I heard the song of an arrow and then I felt the pain in my shoulder. I was pinned to the mast by his knife, and my guns dropped useless to the ground, going off as they fell. I heard him cry and then watched as he pitched out of the sails, plunging head-first into the shallow water.

Because the ship was tipped on its side, I was suspended out over the water. I saw Hands hit the water and then settle on the bottom, dead both from my shot and from the water.

Instead of being relieved, I started to feel very ill and faint. There was blood running down my back and chest. His knife had fastened me to the mast and my arm was starting to feel like it was on fire. What was really bothering me was the fear that I would fall straight down to join Mr. Hands.

I held on to the mast for dear life and closed my eyes to the sight. As I started to calm down, I was able to think about my predicament. I could not dislodge the knife, either from its depth or from my own nerves, and shuddered. That in itself was the answer, for the knife had only pierced a small piece of skin and I was free. Although my blood flowed more freely, I could tell I was basically unhurt and ripped my shirt and jacket free of the knife.

I climbed down, stepped onto the deck, and bound my arm as best as I could. The ship was now mine, and the first thing I did was pitch the dead O'Brien overboard to join Israel Hands. I looked around the ship, watch-

ing the sails flutter in and out with the breeze.

The ship would be damaged with the sails still up, so I quickly lowered the jib sails. The mainsail was harder to maneuver for a portion was actually in the water due to the tilt of the ship. With a great deal of struggle, I finally cut that portion free.

It was now twilight and starting to get cool. Grabbing the cut hawser rope, I jumped to the water, not too far away. It was pretty shallow. I was soon ashore and left the ship as she lay. She was free of the pirates; none of the rest knew where she was. If I could make my way back to the stockade and my comrades, we could have a chance of escaping off this wretched island. Hopefully the capture of the ship would outweigh my desertion and the others would forgive me.

I made my way to the spot closest to where I had first encountered Ben Gunn, walking with great caution as I went. In the darkness, I began to sense a glow in the sky. I pictured the island man cooking his supper over an open fire, but wondered at his foolishness. Surely Silver and his gang would see and sneak up unnoticed.

As the night grew darker, I had a more difficult time. There was no light to guide my path until I saw the moon rise above Spy-glass. The rest of the journey was quickly accomplished and I came to the area close to the thicket. I had to proceed cautiously to avoid being mistakenly shot by my friends.

I could tell a campfire had been lit close to the stockade, although I could not imagine why. As I came closer, I could see the shadow of the log house and an enormous bonfire lit to the side. It was very quiet, with only the barest whisper of a breeze. I could see or hear nothing else.

I had not counted on this. Captain Smollett had ordered us not to build fires, and I was beginning to suspect that something had gone terribly wrong. Maybe they had deserted it.

Crawling around to the eastern side, I crossed to the palisade, where it was darkest, and silently advanced. To my delight, I could hear the sounds of men snoring. I could not believe their watch was so bad! If Silver and his pirates had been the ones advancing, my friends would have stood no chance. Since I knew the captain to be wounded, I swore at myself for leaving them so short of men and poorly defended.

When I reached the door, I stood up and entered. It was so dark I could see nothing inside and heard only the snoring continue.

With my arms outstretched I walked in to surprise my friends. Suddenly a voice rang out: "Pieces of eight! pieces of eight!" The voice continued on as only Silver's parrot could do. I had made a horrible mistake. These men needed no watchman for the parrot was the best one of all.

I heard Silver asking who was there as the rest of the men woke up. As I turned to run, they were lighting a torch and I was caught in the vise-like grip of one of the pirates. I had been captured by Silver and his men.

CHAPTER 12

Nightmare in Real Life

By the light of the torch I saw my worst nightmare had come true. I was in the enemy's camp and did not know where my friends were. The pirates had the provisions and I was afraid my friends had lost the battle and were dead. I was beginning to wish I had died with them.

Six pirates were left, now awake from their drunken slumber. One of them was injured and wore a bloody bandage around his head. I was sure was been the man who had scaled the palisade, been shot by us, and then run away.

Captain Flint was perched on Long John's shoulder and preened himself. Silver did not look the grand pirate captain anymore; his coat was filthy and he was pale in the dim light.

"Well, who've we got here? Jim Hawkins, eh? Just dropped in for a spell? Well, that's perty nice, I'd say!"

Silver sat down and started to fill his pipe. "Well Jim, now's you're here. Let's have a talk. I always thought you were perty smart; you remind me o' myself when I's younger. I's sure didn't 'spect you'd come back, though."

I had no reply, sitting against the wall, surrounded by my worst enemies, more shocked than I had ever been in my life. I tried desperately to hide my feelings and keep calm.

"You're entitled to your fair share o' the treasure. Keep clear o' the Cap'n, he's too strict. The doctor, well, he swore off o' you. Called you a horrible troublemaker. Guess you'll have to join us agin."

Since my friends seemed to no longer want me, and I could not take the ship by myself, I was going to have to join Silver and his gang, at least for the moment.

Silver had told me what I needed to know. My friends still lived and though I believed there to be some truth to Silver's comments about the doctor, I was not too upset. Silver continued, offering me the choice to join or leave, proud of his fairness to me.

"If I'm given the choice to stay or not, I'd like to know what happened to my friends," I replied. "How did you come to be here and where did the others go?"

Silver told me the story. Yesterday, Dr. Livesey had approached Silver with the flag of truce and told him the ship had sailed away. None of the pirates had noticed because they'd been drinking. None had thought the ship would disappear. But Dr. Livesey was right—the ship was gone! Silver admitted that he and his men looked pretty foolish. The doctor had a deal. The pirates were to have the stockade, complete with food, drink, and firewood and the rest were to leave, their lives intact. The doctor's party had been allowed to go, but Silver and his men did not know where. He looked at me again.

"You weren't included in the deal," he said. "There were four leaving, one injured, and he had no idea what had happened to you."

"As for Jim Hawkins," Dr. Livesey had said, "I don't know where he disappeared to and I don't frankly care. He is nothing but a horrible troublemaker. We don't want to see him again."

Now I had to choose and answer Silver.

"I don't care anymore. Whatever happens, happens I say. But let me tell you one thing. Here you sit, most of your men dead, your ship gone, and the treasure still buried. Some success you are! If you want to know who is responsible for your losses, I'll tell you. It was me all along! I heard everything while

you were sitting by the apple barrel. You were talking to Hands and Dick Johnson and now Hands is at the bottom of the sea, thanks to me. I am the one who took your ship away. I cut the cable and killed the men on board. I put her someplace where you will never find her. It's all been me! I'm not afraid of you at all, Silver, and I can hardly wait until I have brought you to court to see you all hang!

"I have one more thing to say. If you leave me alone, I'll save you all. That's the best I can do. Kill me and you are all lost here on this island. Spare me, and I'll be your witness to good. Now you have to choose!"

I stopped, out of breath, and looked at the six of them staring at me speechless. After a moment, I continued.

"Now, Mr. Silver," for I would not call him Captain any longer, "I think you are the best man in this group. I ask only one thing. If things don't work out, please tell the doctor what happened to me, so that he may make up his own mind."

Silver promised he would but in a tone of voice I could not read. I wasn't sure if he was laughing at me or admiring me.

Another man, by the name of Morgan, spoke up, telling the others I was the one who had known Black Dog. Another remembered that I was the one responsible for taking the treasure map from Billy Bones, the captain who had lived at our inn. Soon the rest of the men were ready to kill me.

Silver put a stop to them and threatened their very lives if they harmed me, but the men were still not persuaded.

"Do any o' you want to fight me?" he roared. "I've lived a long time and you're welcome to have it out with me. I'll flay you alive, I promise!"

No one made a move.

"Well, if that's the way you want it. Since you all elected me Cap'n, then that's what I

am. I'm the best sailor here, and you all know it. If you aren't going to fight like true pirates, then you've no choice but to follow what I say! He may be a boy, but he's a sight better man than the rest o' you. Anyone touches him, I'll finish off and that's that!"

No one spoke and the only sound I could hear was my heart pounding in my ears. Silver looked calm and relaxed, but he was watching his men like a hawk, ready to spring if necessary. The rest of the men withdrew to the other side of the log house, whispering among themselves, and looking nervously now and again at Silver.

He finally demanded to know what they were talking about, and one of the men answered for the rest.

"Sorry, sir," he said. "Since you want the rules followed, could you enforce all of 'em? We're mighty tired o' being harassed. We don't like to be bullied. Accordin' to your own rules, we're allowed to talk amongst ourselves.

Beggin' your pardon, sir, we 'us going to step outside for a conference."

Saluting their captain, the men stepped outside, led by the man who had done the talking. He was about thirty-five and looked very yellow and ill. Silver and I were alone.

"Listen, Hawkins," he said in a voice so low I could hardly hear him, "we've got us a problem. These men are more than ready to kill you or torture you. I'll stick with you, no matter what. I hadn't intended to, until you gave that there speech. You're my last hope and I'm yours, that's for sure!"

"Do you mean we are finished?" I asked.

He said we were. When he had looked out to sea and saw the ship was gone, he knew it was only a matter of time. He knew his men to be fools and promised to save my life, but only if I would promise to keep him from a hanging.

"I'll do the best I can," I promised, and the deal was struck.

Lighting his pipe again, he continued.

"You have to understand one thing now, Jim. I've switched to the squire's side. I know you moved the ship somewhere safe, though I can't figures out how. I won't ask hows you did it, or what happened to Hands and O'Brien. And I won't let the men ask you. We 'us finished here. For such a young boy, you've proved your worth."

He poured himself a drink, offering some to me but I refused. Then he asked me the question I could have least expected.

"Do you have any ideas on why that doctor gave me the map, Jim?"

My face provided him with the answer; the question was a total surprise. He shook his large head and looked like a man expecting the worst.

CHAPTER 13

Another
Black Spot

After some time, one of the other pirates came back inside. Saluting Silver, he asked for a torch and took the only torch back outside, leaving Silver and me in the dark.

By the light of the torch outside, we could see the group bent over a book. One of them had his knife out and appeared to be cutting something. Within a few minutes, they started to come our way. When I warned Silver, he did not seem the least bit concerned.

The five pirates entered the room and one came slowly toward us, something held in his hand. Silver gave him encouragement, saying he respected the rules and would hear them out.

The pirate slipped something into Silver's hand, which I could not see. He opened his palm to look. It was a black spot. They had cut a page from Dick's Bible to make the spot.

Silver was more upset that they had cut a Bible than that he had received the black spot. Pirates tend to be very superstitious and he told them they would all hang for sure, because of it. Dick, the Bible's owner, told him to be quiet and reminded him that they had followed the rules. Now Silver was duty bound to obey the time they had specified on the back.

He turned it over and read it. They had fired him from his post. Silver reminded them that he had to hear their complaints and was allowed time to answer them before he would step down.

The pirate, George, who seemed to be their new leader, was not too impressed. He stated their complaints. Silver was told he'd botched the whole cruise and all their plans and would be a fool to admit to anything less. The second point was that he had allowed the captain and the rest to disappear without a trace and they did not know why. The third point was that the pirates had wanted to kill the squire and his company, but Silver had not allowed them. They accused him of wanting to double-cross them and switch sides, joining the captain and his men. The fourth thing concerned me. They were afraid they would all be hung because of Silver's mistakes.

Silver was eager to answer. He reminded them they had already given him a black spot the day we landed. Now they were the ones responsible for the mess they were in, not him. If they had done as he wanted, they would have had the treasure by now. Anderson, Hands, and George Merry, the new leader, had been the instigators of the first spot. They would be the cause of everyone swinging from the Execution Dock in London.

The other pirates' faces were quite a study as they digested Silver's words. He continued to threaten and harangue them and his words started to take effect.

"That was number one," he said. "You make me fair sick you do! Some 'gentlemen of fortune' you are! I know you can see me in your mind's eye swingin' from the scaffold. If you, Merry, Morgan, Hands, and Anderson, hadn't wrecked everything, we'd be sittin' fine by now!"

"I'll tell you about point four," he continued. "In the case of Jim Hawkins here, why he's a hostage, near's I can tell. You idiots would waste a hostage, but not me. For point three, you guys forgot that the doctor is coming to see us each day. He patched you up John, didn't he? And you, George Merry, with the fever makin' your eyes and skin all yellow, don't forget what the doctor's done for you, now! By the way, they're s'posed to be sendin' a consort to fetch us if we don't come back.

Bet you didn't know that, did you? If we have a hostage, we'll have something to bargain with, won't we? But, no, you dimwits would kill him now, and then where would you be?"

He threw down the treasure map onto the floor and the rest of the pirates were on it in a second. They could not have been more excited to see the actual gold. I still could not figure out why the doctor had given it to them. They wanted to know how they were going

to get the treasure home. Silver reminded them again it had been their bungling that had lost the ship. He figured he had all but found the treasure, and since they no longer wanted him, he resigned. Now they could not fire him. They would have to find someone else to do the job.

The pirates all wanted him to be their captain again, and they took back their black spot. Silver tossed it to me. It had been cut out of Dick's Bible, an act Dick now very much regretted. On one side the words of the book of Revelation could still be read, a verse about dogs and murderers roaming the land. I thought it very appropriate. The wood ash they had used was rubbing off, exposing the lettering underneath. The other side had the word "deposed" on it. I have kept that tiny scrap of paper, and still look at it every now and again.

They all had a drink and then retired to bed. Silver made George Merry, the instigator, stand watch and threatened to kill him if he didn't do his job well enough.

I had a hard time sleeping. I kept thinking of all the events that had happened that day, from Hands' death at my hand, to not finding my friends, and to now being a hostage of Silver's. I must admit, Silver gave a marvelous performance, changing the minds of the pirates. He was as cool a character as you'll ever see. He slept like a baby, as if he had no cares in the world, and not like someone who was sleeping with a pack of cutthroats. They could double-cross him in a minute.

In the morning we woke to hear the doctor calling to us. I was eager to see him on the one hand and dreading it on the other. I felt totally ashamed to meet his eye. Silver greeted him eagerly and told him they had a surprise for him. When he found out it was me, it was several seconds before he could respond.

He entered and merely nodded to me before he went to see the rest of the men. He treated them each with respect, although he must have known they could have killed him if they wanted. His professional manner put the men at ease. They acted as if nothing unusual was going on. It was like we were all home, living a normal life, not stuck on some island with a mutiny on our hands.

John's injured head was found to be healing nicely, and Dr. Livesey asked George if he was still taking his medicine. The good doctor

told the men that he intended to do everything he could to keep them alive. He did not want to lose any of King George's men, even if they were bound for the gallows. To that no one made a reply.

He examined Dick and found that he was beginning to suffer from malarial fever. The doctor told them that living in the swamp had brought it on. He thought Silver had better sense than to allow his men to do that. When he had finished, he nodded to me and asked to have a word alone with me. George Merry protested loudly. Silver told him to be quiet and made me promise not to run with the doctor.

I agreed and we would be allowed to step to the stockade walls, the doctor on the outside and me on the inside. After Silver and I left the log house, the pirates continued to protest, swearing at Silver all the time. It was to no avail for he still controlled them.

Silver warned me to go slowly, knowing that the pirates would try to kill me if they thought I was trying to make a break for it. We made our way to the wall. All at once, now that we were out of earshot of the others, his manner changed completely. Now Silver was beseeching the doctor to remember how he had saved my life, acting as if he were afraid of the men in there and was only barely able to control them. Then he left us alone.

The doctor and I discussed my predicament. I started to cry, asking his forgiveness and agreeing that Silver had indeed saved my life. I was afraid only of torture, and the doctor was moved enough to encourage me to try to make a run for it. I told him I had given my word and wouldn't hear of it. I had to stay with Silver for now.

I went on to tell him of the ship, giving him its location and telling him the rest of my story. He marveled at how I had been responsible for saving their lives each time: I had discovered the pirates' initial plans and had found Ben Gunn. Here he stopped for a moment.

He told me that was by far the best deed I had done, and then he shouted to Silver.

"Silver," he cried. "I wouldn't be in too much of a hurry to go after that treasure if I were you!"

Silver said he had to in order to redeem himself and save my life. The doctor warned him to beware of squalls when we found it.

Silver was confused, not understanding either the doctor's warning or why he had been given the map in the first place. The doctor would say no more on the subject. Dr. Livesey did promise that if any of us made it alive through this adventure, he would indeed say a good word on Silver's behalf. The pirate could hope for nothing better.

The doctor warned him to keep me close beside him and to yell if we needed help. He was on his way to get help for us, and so he said goodbye and strode off into the woods.

CHAPTER 14

The Search for
Flint's Fist

Before we went in, Silver made me a promise. He would save my life if I promised to save his. We would be going to search for the treasure. If something happened, he and I were to work together and save both our lives. I didn't really have a choice.

Our breakfast was ready. The pirates had cooked an entire ox, much more than we could finish, but this was their usual habit, wasting firewood, wasting food. The leftovers were tossed in the fire and their careless manner did not offer me much hope about the coming trip. Silver did not berate them for their sloppiness. He talked only of their com-

215

ing success, saying that since they had the small boats, they were likely to be successful.

He told them I would not be allowed to talk to the doctor any more, and he would keep me roped to him as we walked. If I obeyed him and helped, I would be offered my share of the booty, just like everyone else.

He was a master of deception, able and willing to play both sides of the fence. I knew he was totally untrustworthy. I despaired, because I was sure he had only his personal interests at heart and would turn against me in a flash if he had to. I began to wonder what would happen if things turned out alright and Dr. Livesey could not help us escape. What chance did Silver, a cripple, and me, a mere boy, have against the rest of the armed pirates?

On top of all this, I still did not understand what had happened to my friends. They had left the treasure hunting to us and I was confused about the doctor's warning to Silver regarding the squalls.

After breakfast we started off, everyone a sorry sight in soiled clothes and all but me armed to the hilt. I was roped to Silver, who wore two guns, his cutlass, and had two pistols in his pocket. Captain Flint, the parrot, sat on his shoulder and talked incessantly.

The others carried either pickaxes and shovels or our food. They brought the two small boats, now broken and dirty, with us, to enable us to get away if need be.

The chart said the following:

"Find giant tree at base of Spy-glass at N of N. N. E. Look toward Skeleton Island E. S. E. and by E. Walk ten feet. Silver bar is in north spot, look to the lie of east knoll, 60 feet S. of dark cliff with face. Arms easy to find. Go to hill of sand N. point of cape on north cove, E. and a quarter N.

The pirates argued over the chart. Its references were not all that clear; each had his own ideas of which tall tree would be the first marker. Silver just shrugged his shoulders and told them to wait until we got there.

We came to another river that ran down Spy-glass from a forest. We turned to the left and began to climb to the plateau.

The terrain was more difficult until we came to an open plain of flowering plants and bushes. The air was wonderful and affected our spirits, causing the men to be in a very joyful mood. They began to be full of confidence that their mission would be successful. Silver and I brought up the rear. Sometimes I had to lend him a hand, or both of us would have fallen back downhill.

About half a mile further, the pirate in front began to howl in terror. The others quickly ascended to where he was, knowing he certainly hadn't found something good.

Sitting embedded in a vine were the bleached bones of a man, a sailor to be sure

for scraps of his coat were still visible. The sight shocked every one of us. Silver wondered why the bones were laid out in such a way that the arms were pointing directly overhead, as if ready to dive into the water. This was obviously not how he had died.

"I've an idea," he said. "This here fellow's our compass. The top point o' Skeleton Island lies right along. Take a bearing along those bones, now." When they took a bearing on their compass, they found he was right. The compass pointed exactly E. S. E. and by E.

With a shiver, they remembered the reputation of the original Captain Flint. He had gone ashore with six men and had been the only one to come back. This must have been one of the men he killed. Looking at the length of the bones and the yellow hair still visible, they figured it must have been a man called Allardyce. They looked for his possessions, but it appeared as if somebody had already picked the dead man's pockets.

Six had come before, and six they were now. The original six had been killed and they all began to feel as if Flint's ghost were walking nearby, although Morgan had seen him dead with his own eyes. Flint had died a horrible death, and they were afraid his spirit walked yet. His favorite song had been the one about fifteen men and rum. Although they sang it often enough, each man vowed he got a chill when he heard it now.

"Stop this here nonsense!" Silver said. "Dead men don't talk or walk, remember. Especially in the day time. Onward to the treasure!"

He was not afraid of Flint now and never had been. He ordered them on. We started again but without the merry confidence we had before, gone forever by the sight of those bones.

When we reached the top of the hill, the whole party stopped for a rest. We were now high enough to see quite a distance around us.

Over the woods below, we could see the Cape of the Woods and the expanse of sea beyond. At our backs we could see the spot where we had anchored the *Hispaniola* when we arrived and Skeleton Island. To the east was the spit and lowlands, and the sea beyond that. Spy-glass was above us, a hard, rocky summit with a few lonely fir trees. The only sounds came from the far waves breaking upon the rocks and the buzzing of the insects close by. No trace of other humans could be seen.

Silver took our bearings with the compass. He pointed out three "tall trees" in a line from Skeleton Island, and figured the "base of Spy-glass" referred to the point down lower. Such was his confidence that he suggested we have dinner first before going on.

The others were still affected by Allardyce's bones and wanted the whole business done with. Their voices were almost a whisper now, so afraid were they.

Suddenly, from the direction of the trees in front of us, came a high, quavery voice singing Flint's song:

"Fifteen men on the
dead mate's trunk—
Yo-ho-hum, and a bottle full of rum!"

Six men were struck terrified.

"It must be Flint!" exclaimed Merry.

The sound ceased as quickly as it had begun, as if the singer had been silenced by a hand across its mouth. Within our present setting, I thought the song sounded rather pretty, but my companions were frightened out of their wits.

Even Silver was influenced, his face becoming a deathly gray, and he tried to encourage the men to continue. They started to respond but the voice started again, this time among the rocks on Spy-glass.

This time it cried about a man by the name of Darby M'Graw, and something about "fetching some rum." I think the men would have turned and run if there had been somewhere to go. Those had been Flint's last words.

Dick had his broken Bible out and was praying with great fervor. Silver, shaken, would not give in. "Wait a minute!" he said. "The only ones who've heard of Darby is us. Somethin' funny's goin' on here. I want that treasure, and I mean to get it. Nothing's goin' to stop me, not even Flint dead. There's seven hundred thousand pounds sitting less than a quarter of a mile from here. What pirates were ever afraid to get to that much loot?"

Not so easily persuaded this time, the rest of the pirates became even more frightened. "Easy Silver," Merry said. "It's powerful bad fortune to cross a spirit." They clung desperately to Silver in hopes that his courage would sustain them too.

"Somthin's not right here," he said. "If that be a spirit, how come it has an echo. Spirits don't have shadows, do they? Now why

would it have an echo? It don't make sense."
George Merry started to perk up at this and
started to think about the voice. He had heard
Flint's voice, and this was clearly different.

"By gum, that sounds like Ben Gunn's!"
shouted Silver.

"You're right!" shouted Morgan. "That was
Ben Gunn's voice!" None of them could figure
out how Ben Gunn could be on the island. Reassured, they made up their minds that they
were not afraid of the voice any longer,
whether Ben Gunn was dead or alive.

Now they were excited and eager again,
and soon took up their loads and started walking. Only Dick looked worried and continued
to pray with the same fervor, but no one took
any notice. Silver teased him about his Bible,
saying he had brought it on himself.

Dick was beginning to look like he was suf-
fering from the fever. The heat, fatigue, and
shock he had endured were plainly visible to
see, just as Dr. Livesey had predicted.

We walked on, the way easy and pleasant until we reached the first of the tall trees. Taking our bearings, the third one proved to be correct—a tree of immense proportions, visible from the sea to the east and west.

The company was less impressed with its size than with the knowledge that seven hundred thousand pounds of gold lay buried close by. The excitement caused them to forget entirely their previous fear, and their faces grew more animated. In their eagerness, they picked up their pace.

Silver had the worst time of it. He limped, muttering as he went, tugging at my line angrily, looking at me as if he'd like to kill me right then and there. I could see the hatred in his eyes and had no doubts as to his treachery. All earlier promises were forgotten. I was sure he would do whatever was necessary to protect the treasure and seize for himself the greatest portion, or all of it, if the opportunity arose.

It was hard going for me, knowing I was alone. Silver was a traitor, Dick was babbling in delusion brought on by fever, and I was haunted by the memory of the original six.

What tragedy had been caused by this treasure! That terror Flint with his six dead comrades had died a horrible death begging for rum. This peaceful, beautiful forest would have rung with their cries. I was sure I could still hear their voices. We came to the edge of the grove. Merry and the others started to run.

Ten yards ahead, they all stopped. We heard a moan rise from every voice. Silver and I dragged ourselves forward as fast as we could before we came to a complete stop.

We saw a huge pit. It was not very new; the sides were falling in and weeds had started to grow at the bottom. A broken pick lay at the bottom, and a few chests lay broken to the side. I could see the name "Walrus" written on one, the name of Flint's ship.

Somebody had beaten us to it. The seven hundred thousand pounds of gold were all gone, every last piece!

CHAPTER 15

The End of
the Adventure

Their reaction was swift; each man looked as if he'd been hit. Silver took it hard. His very soul had been counting on that money, but he controlled himself and reacted instantly.

He quietly gave me the double-barreled pistol and warned me to look out for trouble. Together we moved to the other side of the pit. He wisely let it be a barrier between the other pirates and ourselves. Now he was acting my friend again, and his constantly changing attitude made me disgusted.

The other five pirates jumped down into the hole, frantically digging with their bare hands, hoping their worst fears were wrong. Morgan was lucky enough to find one piece of gold, but this only made him more furious. They started to swear at Silver, but he stood his ground.

Furious, they crawled out of the pit, fortunately on the other side from us. We all stood, angry and disappointed, but no one willing to take the first shot. I could not believe Silver's courage. He faced the men down, never moving a muscle.

Merry decided to make a speech.

"Men," he said. "There's five o' us and two o' them, and only three legs between 'em. I bet he even knew all along there was nothin' left! We should'a killed the old one a long time ago, and I intend to have the young one's heart myself!"

Just as he was ready to give the order, we all heard the crack of three muskets firing from the bush. Merry was the first to fall, the man with the bandaged head fell next, and the other three turned tail and ran for their lives. Merry was not dead, but Long John fired and finished him off.

Dr. Livesey, Ben Gunn, and Gray came out of the woods. The doctor ordered every one to follow those in retreat. He did not want them to get to the boats first.

Silver was amazing. Hobbling as he was on his crutch, exhausted and disappointed, he still managed to make his way through the chest-high bush to keep up with the rest of us. He had let go of the rope tying us together before. Though he was a good distance behind us, he was the first to notice the three pirates running straight for Mizzen-mast Hill. We were now between them and the boats, so we sat down to rest. Silver thanked Dr. Livesey for saving our lives and greeted Ben Gunn. Gray went back to retrieve the pickaxes and the rest of us strolled casually down to the boats. Ben Gunn told Silver what had happened to him.

Ben, alone on the island, had found the skeleton and had picked the pockets. He had found the treasure and dug it up, carrying it on his back to a cave on the northeast part of the island. The job had taken him many months, but he had finished the task about two months before we had come with the *Hispaniola*.

The doctor had learned this from Ben the afternoon the stockade was attacked. When he had found the ship gone the next morning, he gave the map to Silver, since it was of no use to him any longer. Ben Gunn had ample supplies of food, so the rest of my friends had turned the loaded stockade over to Silver's men. They wanted to get away from the unhealthy swamp and be able to guard the money.

When the doctor found out I was a hostage of the pirates, he had returned to the others to get help. The squire was left behind to guard the captain and he, Gray, and Ben Gunn had come to our rescue.

We were too far ahead for them to reach us, so Ben Gunn, familiar to the island, had been sent ahead to play tricks on the pirates' superstitions. He had been the one singing as the pirates had eventually guessed. Because Silver had kept me so close to him, my life was saved in the fight.

When we reached the boats, Dr. Livesey destroyed one completely. We boarded the other one to go to Ben Gunn's cave. Eight or nine miles around to the North Inlet, even Silver was told to man one of the oars. The poor man was nearly exhausted. With all of us pulling, we passed the distance quickly.

We passed the hill near to Ben Gunn's cave and could see a figure leaning on a gun, guarding the entrance. Waving a handkerchief and giving three cheers, we greeted the squire. Silver cheered with as much enthusiasm as the rest.

Just inside the North Inlet, we came upon the *Hispaniola*, sailing by herself! She had been lifted with the last heavy rain. We were quite lucky there were no strong winds or currents to carry her away. Except for the damage to the mainsail inflicted by myself, she was fine. We managed to drop another anchor from her and she was berthed where she was. We rowed to Ben Gunn's place, and Gray was sent back in the boat to spend the night on board the *Hispaniola*.

The squire met us close to the entrance of the cave. He greeted me kindly, saying nothing of what I had done. When Silver saluted smartly at him, he became flustered.

"John Silver, you are a monstrous scoundrel and a total hypocrite. I have been told I cannot charge you; therefore, I will not. You will have to live with the dead men hanging from your neck for the rest of your life."

Silver thanked the squire, but the man wanted no part.

We went into the cave and found it a most pleasant place, with its own spring and ferns growing beside it, and a comfortable sand floor. A big fire was burning, and Captain Smollett was laying close by. By the light of the fire, we could see, far at the back, an immense pile of gold coins and bars from the treasure.

I wondered at how many men had lost their lives over this fortune. We had suffered loss, and Flint's voyage had lost men. How many more had lost their lives as this hoard was being collected? How many had walked a plank, or been shot, or betrayed? No one would ever know. And yet, three men still alive had been part of this treachery: Silver, Morgan, and Ben Gunn, each hoping for his share of the profits.

The captain greeted me warmly, complimenting me on my bravery, but saying he would prefer not to have me aboard the next time he sailed. He was surprised to see Silver, but Silver answered, "A job is a job, sir. I'm only doin' me duty."

Nothing more was said, and we settled down to our supper. Silver celebrated with us, serving each of us in turn, doing his best to look the faithful servant.

The next morning, the job of moving the gold to the *Hispaniola* got underway. It was nearly a mile to the beach from the cave, and three miles by boat to the ship. We did not worry about the three pirates still on the island and posted a single guard on the hill.

Gray and Ben Gunn did the boating, and the rest of us lent our backs to the carrying. The bars were so heavy that two of them made one load. Since I was the smallest, I packed the coins into bags.

It was some collection; as diverse as Billy Bones's hoard, but so much larger than I could have imagined. I quite enjoyed the sorting, finding English, French, Spanish, and Portuguese coins of all denominations for the last hundred years. I would find the odd Oriental coin, or pieces with holes in the middle for a rope. By the end, my back ached with their weight as I lifted and bagged them all. The work took several days, and it sometimes seemed the pile would never end.

The third night the doctor and I were walking along the hill overlooking the rest of the island. The quiet was suddenly broken by the sound of men either screaming or singing. Pausing, we looked at each other and realized it was the three pirates who had run away. Silver came up behind us and figured they were drunk.

Silver had been allowed to live freely among us, although he was the recipient of many small insults. He ignored them all and was always polite. Only Ben Gunn treated him differently, for he was still afraid of him. I did not trust him at all, having seen his many changes of heart, and I wavered between distrust and gratitude for saving my life.

That evening, listening to the pirates, the doctor and Silver talked a little while longer.

They wondered whether the pirates had indeed found some rum or whether they had all succumbed to the malaria of the island. Silver did not think they were of any concern to us, either way.

The doctor rounded on him, telling Silver that if they were delirious from the fever, he would try to help them if he could, regardless of the cost to himself.

"I beg your pardon, sir," replied Silver. "If you went down to them, they would kill you for sure, whatever their state. Then we would be the ones to suffer your loss, and our party would be weaker. They are incapable of keeping their word; you don't owe them a thing."

"Oh," replied the doctor. "You are the one to keep your word, aren't you?"

We heard no more from the three. One time we heard a gunshot far off, but that was all. We held a meeting, and it was voted that we desert them on the island. Ben Gunn was delighted; Gray was in agreement. We left behind a large amount of powder and shot; most of Ben Gunn's salted goat meat; some medicine, tools, and clothing; a spare sail; some rope and some tobacco. We left no rum.

Once we got the treasure safely aboard, we packed enough goat meat and water on the ship to last us through any further adventures.

We weighed anchor one beautiful morning, flying proudly the Union Jack that had flown above the stockade.

Coming through the narrows, we found evidence of the three pirates. They must have been watching us for we saw them kneeling on the sand spit, their hands folded in supplication. All of us were moved, but we could not trust they would not mutiny again if we brought them on board. And they would have faced only the hangman's rope if we had taken them home. As we sailed past, they continued to call upon us, begging for God's mercy.

When they saw we were not going to stop, one of them whipped his musket to his shoulder and fired. It went right over Silver's head and into the mainsail. We took cover for a while, but once we had passed out of their range, we feared them no more. Before noon, the island had disappeared to my great joy.

Since we were so few men, everyone had to help. The captain had to lie on deck and issue his orders. He was much better, but we could not risk his health. We headed for the nearest port on Spanish South America. We could not sail the whole way home without some more men. We had a rough time with several gales, leaving us nearly exhausted before we reached port.

We anchored in a port, and were surrounded by boats full of dark-skinned men and others of Mexican Indians. They offered us fruits and vegetables and we were eager to taste the wonderful tropical delights. What a contrast to what had happened on the island, to have the merry faces surrounding us.

The doctor, squire, and I were strolling on the dock one night and met the captain of an

English man-of-war. He invited us on board his ship to talk. It was daybreak before we got back to the *Hispaniola*.

We found Ben Gunn alone on board. Silver had gone, taking with him one of the bags of gold. Ben Gunn had aided him, apologizing, but saying he was not sure of our safety if Silver had remained with us. We thought we had done well to get rid of Silver so easily and cheaply.

The rest of the journey was uneventful. We took on a few more hands and sailed home, reaching Bristol just as Mr. Blandly was beginning to think about coming after us. Only five of our original number came back. The song was right: "Booze and the devil had finished every last one!"

We divided the treasure, and it was used according to our natures, some wisely and some foolishly. Captain Smollett no longer sails and has retired. Gray saved his funds and studied to become a mate. He now owns part

of a fine ship and is a father. Ben Gunn spent most of his money within twenty days and came begging for more. He was given a house to keep and still lives in the country, singing in the church choir.

We never heard from Silver again. Perhaps he met up with his wife, and they live in comfort on the islands, with Captain Flint, the parrot. He will find no haven here.

The silver bar and arms are still on the island, and that is why I have not given its location. We want no part of them; nothing could make me return. I still dream about the sea, the waves, and that dreaded parrot screeching in my ear:"Pieces of eight! Pieces of eight!"